When Stars Collide

Three Novelettes by

Malania E. Reynolds

THREE SKILLET

WHEN STARS COLLIDE, Reynolds, Malania E.

First Edition

 THREE SKILLET

www.ThreeSkilletPublishing.com

Cover design by Farley L Dunn

ISBN: 978-1-943189-33-5

When Stars Collide

A Soldier's Tale

— 1 —

Becca Rains swept from the ballroom and slipped into the darkened library just in time. The barest outlines of shelves bordered the marble mantle, which gleamed briefly as she closed the door. The smell of cognac and pipe smoke mixed with the mustiness of old tomes that were read far too seldom. She ran to a corner near the fireplace and brought her hand to her chest to calm her labored breathing. The thick fabric of her dress rustled as she moved, and she tried to hold very still. She heard the door opening, and there were her mother and Mrs. Elizabeth Fizgibbons in full sail. She stood as still as a tree in winter as her mother's voice penetrated the dim shadows with its shrill, excited and droll exclamation.

"Drat, that girl! I was sure she came in here. I don't know what I'll do, for her father's determined to get her married this season. He's told me he won't expend the funds for another. She's past her twentieth birthdate. It's beyond frustrating that the girl won't settle down to a life of ease and provide heirs for the family. I'd thought tonight when I introduced her to Captain Lankford, she'd see the benefits of marriage to such a handsome and respected man."

"Yes, Maggie, I know just the feeling, for my Druscilla was the same. It took her younger sister, Prudence, coming out the next year that pushed her over the brink, for I'm sure she would've postponed the matter if she hadn't known that we wouldn't tolerate two debutantes lingering longer in an unwed state. If a girl isn't married before she's twenty, society looks at her with disfavor. The expense of new frocks and shoes is daunting for two girls at a time. It's not to be borne."

Becca could sense a strong, large presence behind her, and she froze. She missed the remainder of her mother's conversation as a hard, male arm grasped her around the shoulders and a hand clapped itself over her mouth. The skin was warm and moist, and very, very male. She heard the women leave the room and tried to turn into the arms of her captor, but he held her tight.

"Don't scream, and I'll release my hand from your mouth."

She could feel his breath brush against the hair on her neck as he whispered in her ear, and she shivered. The smell of tobacco and hair tonic tweaked her nose. In the dimness, her eyes could barely make out the objects in the room. As her eyes adjusted to the darkness, she could just decipher the portrait of a soldier on a horse over the fireplace and the floor globe she'd once twirled on an earlier social call, dreaming of places she might one day visit.

She nodded her head, uncertain whether she'd been rescued, or if she was about to be taken advantage of.

Slowly, his hand dropped from her face and he released her. She turned, stepped back and almost tripped over her skirts. He was very tall, and she could see that he didn't have a beard. He was in the dress uniform of a Cavalry officer. She pressed her hand against his breast and pushed hard, but he didn't separate from her. He laughed softly.

"What are you about, Sir? You frightened me. Didn't you see my mother was searching for me? I easily might have called out and compromised myself with a man in a dark room. I'm sure she would have instantly fallen to the opinion that we were having a lover's tryst. And, then you would have made the situation worse."

"Aye, it's so, Miss Rains. I didn't think of the consequences of my actions. I thought only to silence you in case you had the unhappy thought of screaming as you felt my presence."

He withdrew from the dark corner and went toward the lamp near a window and lit it, illuminating Becca's pale blue dress and her graceful frame. Her dark hair shimmered, matching her chocolate brown eyes. Her curls were tied on top of her head with a blue ribbon, with two twisted ringlets hanging in front of her right ear. Her cheeks were on fire with embarrassment and shock.

"Oh, don't do that. They'll see the light, come in and find us here. Wait, how do you know my name?" Becca looked more carefully at the soldier. She saw the twinkle in his eyes as he came closer to her. "Oh, my. Oh, Jerusalem. You're Captain Lankford, the very man I've been running from all evening. I must leave the room at once."

She took a step forward, but he drew her into his arms and kissed her sharply on the lips. She shrank from the attack, and then yielded as she felt a thrill of pleasure race through her. His arms were strong and powerful. He released her and stepped back, a question in his eyes. Did he expect her to scream? She wouldn't, not for a man such as this, no matter what he did. She opened her eyes wide, intensely aware that her breath was racing.

"Please, Sir, I must go in case someone discovers us here." Once more, she turned to leave, but he grasped her arm and stopped her.

"But, I want to be found with you. It's such a stimulating sensation to be caught with a young damsel in my arms. I've grown bored with the tameness of society life of late." His eyes sparkled mischievously in the lamplight, and his lips teased with a smile.

"Are you crazy? You'd have to marry me or be forced to fight a duel for your honor." Becca brought herself out of the fog his kiss had passed over her mind. "Why would you want to be caught with me?" She was more curious than frightened at the idea. Besides, in the light, she found his features more than pleasant.

"Were you not hiding from me? You've admitted as much. Don't you desire to marry me? I'm of the opinion you had set your cap for me and were quite eager for the marriage night to begin. Your mother just confirmed that she and your father approve of the match. Come, stay with me and enjoy the blending of our bodies together."

As he spoke, Captain Lankford guided Becca toward a red brocade sofa near the fireplace. The arms were low, and gleaming wood bordered the back, with curved legs jutting from tassels along the front. The seat sloped gently, perfect for a lovers' rendezvous. He pushed gently, and she collapsed in a heap of skirts onto the surface. He fell on top of her and started kissing her mouth as his hand crept toward the hem of her frock.

Becca was in a quandary. She wanted the kisses to go on, but she knew she must stop him before it was too late. She squirmed and fought, but he was too strong. The roughness of his palm stroked the inside of her thigh, and a warmth rose inside her. She raised her arms to his head and ran her fingers through the softness of his hair. Her lips tingled as he drew back and looked into her eyes.

Unexpectedly, the moment was shattered, and

he was up and moving away from her. He turned and straightened his clothing, tugging at his sleeves and adjusting his collar. He stared at the wall for a moment, his cheeks flushed with red and his eyes shining. She jumped up and pulled her skirts down, adjusted the lace of her bodice and ran her hand over her hair to smooth it. She was almost overwhelmed with the thought of what had happened. She was surprised to hear him sigh with regret. She'd expected a laugh of triumph.

"My God, what have I done?" He pulled a kerchief from his inside pocket and patted his forehead, then nervously attempted to slip it back inside, couldn't seem to find the pocket, and held it wadded in his hand. He looked at her, his face twisted with remorse. "Please, forgive me, Miss Rains. I'll speak to your father as soon as possible." He left the room, opening the door quietly and looking through in a quick glance before disappearing, even before Becca could respond.

Oh, Jerusalem, she thought. I'm compromised, and he thinks he must marry me. Angrily, she stepped to a small looking glass near the door and viewed her hair. One of her curls was out of place. She lifted it, reattached a barrette and was satisfied. She pinched her cheeks to bring up her full color and elevated her chin, thinking, I refuse to marry a man so impulsive. I'll tell father that he doesn't suit me. I'll say that I cannot abide the harshness of a soldier's life. She knew that was a lie as she returned her glance to the looking glass.

She looked alright, only her cheeks were a little pink—and not from her having pinched them—and her eyes were too bright and threatened to weep. With her dress rustling, she slowly and thoughtfully blew out the lamp and walked to the door. She felt the knob, imagining she could feel the hand that had so rudely accosted her still pressed to it, and her heart pounding, she bolted from the room.

Once on the other side of the door, she stopped and braced herself. Nothing had changed. The tall, coffered ceiling with its hammered tin inserts, the damask wallpaper running from floor to ceiling, even the grand chandeliers with their flickering tapers were as she'd left them. The stairway winding up the far wall and the vast stained glass panels on the landing still gleamed with the cheery mood of the festivities. The orchestra was playing a waltz melody, and the dancers were moving around the room as they had been before she'd left the ballroom. She searched for her father, hoping beyond hope he would rescue her from this awful situation but didn't find him. She turned and there was her mother, coming across the room leading a man in a Cavalry uniform. Becca turned away, as she tried to calm her racing heart, and hoped her cheeks weren't as flushed as they felt. It was Captain Lankford, here to greet her as if nothing had happened. She should have never pinched them. Never. She had only made matters worse.

"There you are, Rebecca. I've looked for you

everywhere. But, it's of no importance, for I've come to introduce Captain William Lankford to you. He's expressed a desire to dance with you." Her mother took her elbow and turned her to face the captain.

Her mother seemed so eager and excited that Becca didn't have the heart to disappoint her. It would be a scene, otherwise; and with all her friends and her parents' acquaintances watching, there was nothing to be done. She allowed herself to be led onto the dance floor, where she again felt the sensation of this man's strong arms about her. She took a deep whiff of the familiar tobacco and hair tonic.

"I'm sorry, Miss Rains. I was trying to find your father but was approached by your mother instead. What could I say but that I would be pleased to make your acquaintance?" He paused and glanced at her. He seemed concerned, and her heart skipped a beat. "Have you recovered from your ordeal? I must apologize again for my uncouth and rude behavior. It was unforgivable. I was angry and slightly drunk, I believe, to think that such an opportunity had come my way to pun-ish you for taunting me. It's not often that I'm told that a young lady of your upbringing is eager for my caresses, and then she runs from the sight of me. It was most confusing." Lankford took her arms, and they joined in the familiar steps.

As he held her, Becca responded with equal transparency and a bit of bite. "It's most confusing, as you say, Captain. When my mother approached me with her plans for our marriage, I panicked. I had no thoughts of spending my days as a soldier's widow before I've experienced life." She let the words drip with sarcasm, and the captain looked sharply at her.

"A widow? You see yourself as a widow before we're married? Haven't you considered the glamor and the honor of the army life? I've seen girls swoon from the sight of my men on horseback, riding in review across the parade grounds. They don't think of becoming widows." He twirled her to the sound of music amid the steps of the other dancers. They were separated for a time, and when they came together again, he leaned close and spoke quite sharply. "I was told by an interested party that you are quite fast and loose with your charms. Is this not so, then? Have you not been with a man before tonight?" He stopped and looked at her hard as if daring her to answer, even as the music continued, and the dancers around them progressed in their steps. He was jostled from behind by another dancer, forcing him to continue the dance. They moved with the music, following the formal steps of the dance in silence.

Becca's thoughts were in turmoil, and if she weren't in a crowd of people who would see her and think her mad or worse, she might allow herself to cry. Who could have said such a cruel thing about her, and why? Yet, he had his hand on her arm, and their feet continued to move as if no words had been said. They switched partners, and Becca smiled at the new faces, going through the motions as if in a dream, catching sight of the candles flickering on the walls, with the sounds of taffeta and hard-soled shoes driving her own. Then, he was back, his words in her ears.

"I think we should have this discussion at a more appropriate time. Tomorrow, perhaps. I'll call on your father, and if he permits me, I'll speak with you about our marriage vows." The music stopped, and Becca's heart pounded. A voice, somewhere, tittered with laughter, but it wasn't hers. A man replied, "That was the most enjoyable dance." Yet, from Captain Lankford, there was only silence. He walked her stiffly to her mother's side without allowing her to answer his accusations. His grip on her arm was firm, and she dared not make a sound. He released her, bowed low, and with a series of quick steps, his boots tapping briskly on the parquet, he left the room.

"Daughter, I saw how Mr. Lankford leaned in to you. What did he say? I think I could claim love there, if for the sake of the dance, if nothing other. How do you like him?" Maggie Rains placed her cheek next to her daughter's and gave her a peck of a kiss. She was flushed with her excitement, and her words continued. "He's so handsome, I must say. You must have made quite an impact for him to run away so quickly."

"We spoke briefly, Mama. Nothing more."

Becca fanned her heated face and tried to calm her mother's excitement. "I think I will try my footwork with another man." If she accepted a few more dance partners, she might throw suspicion away from her. She smiled at an officer in his full regalia, and he stepped in her direction. She offered her hand and was swept onto the floor. Soon she was laughing in pretend gaiety, and later, when the music ended, she fled, appalled at her false bravado, only to find herself surrounded by her mother's elderly friends.

She laughed at the ladies' jokes, and as soon as she could make her way through the crowd, she found her parents, said a gracious farewell to her hostess and exited the grand house in the quiet of the early morning hours. She rode in silence in the closed carriage, with her shawl tightly wrapped around her shoulders, while her parents discussed the pursuits of the night. The repetitive sound of the horses' hooves was a background drumbeat keeping her heart in motion, as she worried over the events of the following morning. She hoped beyond hope the evening would be forgotten, and Captain Lankford would never darken her parents' door. She barely registered that her father had won a big pot of money playing whist and felt quite pleased with the turn of events. Her mother seemed distracted and didn't come to her room to discuss Gladys Kitchum's ball.

Becca tossed and turned through the rest of the night and couldn't rest. She moved to the window several times and looked out at the moonlit scene before her. She wished she could ride a horse or take a long walk in the park and escape her thoughts. Or, remove her clothing and swim in the river behind their house; anything, to take her mind from the remembrance of her time in the library with Captain Lankford. She felt again the sensations of being underneath him on the sofa, his hand on her thigh and his tongue as he thrust it into her mouth. She felt warm, then cold, as she realized she had come alive in his arms. Was this the way her mother felt when she slept beside her husband? She supposed it was, else no children would be born into the world. Suddenly, she sat up in bed, her decision made; and drawing the linens once again over her, she snuggled in the warmth of the mattress and giggled under her bedcovers.

— 2 —

Becca rose early but couldn't eat. Her mother had slept late as usual. As soon as she heard her father's voice in the hallway, she thought of going to him with an explanation of her actions in advance of Captain Lankford's possible arrival, but what could she say?

She waited and gazed at the clock until she heard the servant answer the chime of the doorbell and knew that Captain Lankford had arrived. Her heart beat loudly in her chest, and she changed her shawl for the fourth time in nervous anticipation, a pink one to a blue, then to a cream-colored one, and back to the pink. Would he come to her, or would her father toss him out in anger and disgust? She sat with her hands clasped in her lap for what seemed an hour, before she heard the soft tap at her door, announcing the arrival of the servant with the summons to her father's side.

She walked calmly and gracefully down the

stairs, barely noticing the grand, arched window at the landing, covered by her mother's specially-ordered lace curtains which bathed her in a dappled light. The handrail was deepest walnut, shined to a glossy sheen. An emerald runner was bound to the steps with brass rods fastened on each end, and patterned silk wallpaper in a peacock motif whispered behind family portraits in elaborate gold frames. She knocked on the carved library door and was bid to enter by her father's resonate voice. She took a deep breath and walked into the room. Bookshelves circled the space, none reaching higher than her waist, with her father's hunting trophies clambering for attention above. Windows on either side of the ornate mantle were darkened by half-closed shutters. Candles burned angrily on lampstands throughout the room. Sylvester Rains sat behind his desk, his countenance disturbed; his hair mussed as though he'd raked his fingers through it many times. He frowned at her and glanced away.

She turned her eyes toward the captain but couldn't look him in the eyes. He stood straight and tall in his uniform, his gold buttons and braids making him appear quite distinguished. He held his hat in his hand, properly deferential in her father's presence, and his attention on him. The room was so quiet, the tick of the big clock in the hallway was as church bells in her ears. She shut the door softly behind her.

"Yes, Papa. You wanted to see me?" She took

a few steps and thought suddenly how old her father seemed today, not at all as he had last night, bragging over his win at cards.

"Come in, Daughter, and sit down." He leaned back in his chair for a moment, as if considering the situation.

As she slipped carefully into the chair near Captain Lankford, her father said, "Captain, if you please."

The captain filled the chair next to Becca as her father rose and started pacing the room. He looked for a time out the window, but Becca was certain he wasn't seeing the busy activity outside. She felt uncomfortable, with the captain now calmly sitting in the chair beside her, awaiting his fate. She wondered what he'd said to her father, and she shifted her weight. The action seemed to bring her father out of his thoughts, and he turned and looked at first one then the other. He thrust his fingers through his hair, moved to the desk and sat heavily in his chair. He sighed.

"Daughter, Captain Lankford has admitted that he has used you in an improper manner, and that you didn't object. Is that true?" He tapped his fingers on his desktop, the sound as of a ticking clock that counted down the seconds, whether to something good or bad was unclear.

His eyes pierced her soul, and she couldn't deny that she'd felt pleasure during their time on the sofa. She glanced quickly at the captain, but he sat stiff and straight and didn't move. She decided the time had come to put her plan in motion. Whatever had gone on between the men in their discussions couldn't be helped, but she would have her way in this.

"Yes, Papa, it's quite true. I enjoyed the captain's attentions well. I should like to experience it again, many times. I admit that I was shameless in his arms and don't regret it."

As though a gunshot had gone off in the room, the captain jerked and rose to his feet. Likewise, Rains rose so abruptly that his chair almost toppled onto the floor. He righted it with his hand and stared at his wayward daughter.

"Rebecca, are you saying this to disturb me, or to save the captain from guilt? I cannot believe that you would willingly accept the advances of a stranger, and at a public ball, besides, where anyone might have seen you. Please, tell me it isn't so." Rains caught her eyes and held them, but she didn't turn away from his wrath.

"I'm telling the truth, Father. Captain Lankford is a most charming man, and I couldn't resist his kisses." She smiled at the soldier, but he remained steadfastly silent during the interrogation.

"That's enough. I'm ashamed of you, Daughter, that you would admit such wanton behavior. You must be married at once, for God knows, there may already be a child on the way, and we mustn't allow society to feed on your disgrace. I'll send a note to the minister, with your permission,

Sir, and set a date for the marriage immediately. I sorrow for your mother. It's beyond doubt that this will cause talk, but at least we may be able to save your mother from the worst of those who gossip. We must move quickly, in the hope that perhaps people will believe our haste is because of your military obligation." He turned to the desk, searching for paper and a pen.

The captain cleared his throat. "I should like to talk to Miss Rains, if I may, sir, for I must have her personal thoughts about our future life together."

"What is this?" Sylvester Rains turned from his desk with a frown. He erupted in a tirade, revealing his true irritation with the matter at hand. "You dare to ask for time alone with my daughter after such a disgusting display of behavior betraying the uniform you wear? No, I won't allow it. Prepare yourself, Captain, for my wrath and my disgust. You have dishonored your name and your country. I leave it to you to settle the matter with the authorities over you, but as for me and my family, we will provide the means for you to assume your rightful place as my daughter's husband, but that is as far as we will go. Please leave my home immediately. I'll send a note to your quarters when I've organized the plans for the ceremony." He stood behind the desk as though to use it to protect himself from doing bodily harm to his enemy.

Becca watched in wonder as the captain meekly wished them both a good day and left, his shoulders held rigid and his head high. She began to regret her dishonesty, for she should've known that her father would treat him harshly. They hadn't gone to the point of no return, and the captain had stopped his assault when he realized the magnitude of the scene. She thought him a magnificent sight and began to chastise her father as soon as he left the house.

"Papa, you have no call to treat the captain in such a manner." She'd only meant to get a small measure of revenge for the captain thinking her a loose woman. She must be plain and tell her father the entire truth without delay. "I was a willing participant in last night's escapade, and he has come to you as any decent, honorable man would do to ask for your pardon and permission for the marriage. You've assumed the matter went further than it did. We had only a few moments of time and didn't engage in anything beyond a few kisses and caresses." She twisted her hands and appealed to his mercy.

"That's beside the issue. What's done is done and cannot be undone. You've played your childish games one time too often. It shan't happen again, not under my roof. I shudder to think what would have happened if your mother had seen you in the room. What if her friends had come in while you were engaged in such an activity? It doesn't matter. The captain has disgraced himself and you. You've belittled yourself and your name. Leave me. I won't speak of this again. As soon as can be, prepare yourself for a life of marriage and child-birth. Once you are wed, you're no longer welcome in this house."

He again seemed to be looking for paper and a pen. He didn't look up again, as Becca tried to undo the mangled damage to her reputation. She'd never intended something so dramatic.

"But, Father—" He turned his back, and she knew he wouldn't listen to her. She ran up the stairs and knocked on her mother's door.

"Yes, dear, who is it?"

"Becca, Mama. Are you presentable?" She kept one hand on the knob and another on the doorframe, with barely a sliver of space to speak through.

"Sweetheart, come in. Good morning, and how is your day going?"

Becca opened the door to find her mother was still in bed, eating a slice of bread from a tray. She waved in greeting to her daughter, motioning to her to come closer, and she lifted her chin for a kiss. Becca pushed her despair aside long enough to give the expected kiss, then her anguish came pouring forth.

"Mama, it's all come undone. Papa says I must marry Captain Lankford, and the man has gone to inform his superiors of his approaching marriage. We haven't time to spare. I must have my hair done, and a dress prepared, for Papa won't wait." She dropped to sit on her mother's bed, grasping her mother's hand and pressing it to her cheek. She didn't know whether to cry or not to. She'd wanted this, certainly, but not in this manner; and her father had been so very angry. What would she do?

"What? You're to marry Captain Lankford after all? Oh, this is good news. What's this about a dress? Of course, child, we shall have the seamstress prepare your wedding clothes." Maggie kissed her daughter's hand, threw her coverlet and bedding aside, and rose from the bed to ring for her maid.

"We don't have time for the seamstress, Mama. We're to be married immediately, Papa says; as soon as the preacher can come and the license bought. Oh, I've made a muddle of it all; I only meant to tease him a little; but Papa's turned his back on me." Becca stood at the window, looking out over the lawn, with the large, spreading trees shading the lush grass. The sun fell against her skin, warm and comforting. She would miss this. She'd never thought so, but now that the prospect was upon her, and with her father's angry words, she might never see it again. It was a rock in her stomach, and she didn't think it could be borne.

"Immediately? But, we must have time to prepare. What's going on that you must be married so quickly?" Maggie stopped speaking as the maid came in to take the tray away. She looked longingly at the food, but let it be carried from the room without protest. As soon as the maid had left, she cautiously opened the door to make sure no one could overhear their conversation. "My word, child, my hair. I must prepare for the day. No doubt we shall be very busy. My robe, hand it to me."

Becca lifted the heavy wool robe from the back of a chair and held it to her mother. Maggie pulled it over her shoulders, and now dressed, she sat at the dressing table to brush her hair. She lifted one brush to find it full of hair, muttered something, picked up another, and began to pull it through her hair.

"Mama, do you remember last night when you and Elizabeth Fitzgibbons came into the library?" Becca took the brush and began to brush her mother's hair for her. Her mother nodded her head and gazed at her daughter through the looking glass.

"Yes, dear, but no one was inside." She smiled as if in apology for not having more information.

"Mama, the captain and I were in the shadows of the room, near the fireplace. His arms were around me holding me tightly."

"Becca!" As though a spring had popped from the cushion of her stool, Margaret Rains twisted to face her daughter, knocking the brush from her hand. She gaped at Becca in shock.

"We made love on the sofa near the fireplace after you left." She might as well say it. Her father already believed it. It sounded worse than horrible spoken aloud. "Father's decided that we must be married immediately to quail the gossips. He fears the news will get out that we behaved wantonly during the ball. The captain and he have had a talk in the library, and he sent Captain Lankford away in disgrace. Please, forgive me for telling you before you finished your repast, but I could wait no longer. Papa will no doubt be here in a few moments to explain the plans he's made for the future."

"Becca, I do declare!" Her mother had no other words and simply stared at her in surprise as her eyes turned red and tears began to roll down her face.

Becca backed slowly from the room and quietly closed the door, her thoughts in turmoil and leaping haphazardly from one disastrous thought to another. She hadn't considered the consequences of her foolish actions. She should've waited until her father explained to her mother in private. She shouldn't have admitted her guilt. She should've denied the attentions of the Cavalry officer and helped him through the ordeal. Instead, she'd made it worse, and now he would pay for her sins.

She felt no inclination to blame him for his attempted conquest. It infuriated her that someone had suggested she was easy and wanton, but if he'd heard such news, he would have been equally surprised to have her refuse him. Then, making matters worse, she'd participated in her own disgrace by suggesting the deed had been consummated.

The thing that puzzled her most was this: What motive would her friends have for telling the captain such horrendous things about her? Oh, Jerusalem. She was in a situation over which she no longer had control. She covered her face and ran down the hallway, blinded by her tears.

"He'll never forgive me," she told the painted portrait of her grandparents on the wall, but the smiling couple didn't answer her.

— 3 —

The marriage was arranged quietly and quickly, and before the new bride-to-be's boxes and trunks were completely packed and on their way to the captain's barracks at the Army post, the society gossips were spreading the news abroad that Rebecca Rains was with child. It was impossible, of course, for he hadn't been with her beyond the disastrous few moments in the library on the night of Gladys Kitchum's ball. The more she tried to deny the charges, the worse the gossip progressed, and finally Becca became silent and no longer tried to save her reputation.

There were only a few hasty flowers set up in the parlor, a few roses from the hothouse and several chrysanthemums from the cook's pot in the kitchen window. A fire crackled in the fireplace, and the room seemed cheery enough, except for the expressions on the faces of those participating. The minister wore a white robe with red vestments and a small cap on his head. His face was solemn and grave as he pronounced the wedding vows. The only persons attending the couple were Becca's parents and Lankford's commanding officer, Colonel James Truitt. Lankford and his officer were in their formal military outfits, with revolvers and sabers on their belts, and their hats jauntily removed, but still dashing with their feathered crowns. Their black boots shined in the gleam of the fire. Once the deed was done—entirely too quickly for Maggie's taste—coffee and small iced cakes were served. After only a short time of awkward congratulations and strained conversation, the participants left; and the house on Brinker Street settled into the long and uncomfortable silence of a lonely winter afternoon.

William and Becca's quarters at the post were mean, rude rooms by the standard of Becca's upbringing. With low ceilings, roughly plastered walls, painted wood floors, and no curtains or shutters on the windows, it seemed little better than a barn. One small room held a cotton mattress on an iron frame, but there was barely room to get from one side to the other without crawling across the bed. The living space was little better, with a desk consuming much of the floor, and only a little sitting area off to the side. The larger portion of Becca's hastily packed luggage was placed in a storage room on the post, and she brought out only those things that would make their small rooms presentable. One positive note proved to be the small fireplace, which at first seemed laughable to Becca, but was quite sufficient to heat the room to a fair temperature, only lacking on the coldest of mornings.

Their first night together was a mixture of despair and passion, the levels of which Becca had truly not expected. Even so, when it was done, she still had the rough wooden floors at her feet, a bed that was little better than a castoff, and no one to iron her clothes or mend her loose hems. In the morning, the captain was up before light and, by a single candle, began to dress.

"William," Becca queried sleepily, "it's the morning after our marriage. Must you leave so early?"

"I have my duties at the post," he answered in a brusque manner. "You have yours, now. I have a patrol I'm assigned to, and we leave today. Don't expect me to return for several weeks." He pulled on his coat, blew out the candle, and was gone, without a word of goodbye or a kiss of affection.

Once Becca's tears were dried, she rose, pulled out her most durable clothes, spent a great deal of time clumsily building a fire in the fireplace, and began to scrub the rooms. The weeks until William returned were lonely, and she often despaired that she had brought this on herself; but with some practice, she learned to cook simple meals and ate alone when not required to attend the formal officers' gatherings. She settled into her quiet life with as much good grace as possible, soon met the other officers' wives and entertained in her limited way. Relationships were strained between the couple, as they each felt guilt over their coming together in such a haphazard way.

For many weeks, Becca pondered the events of the ball and its aftermath and finally decided to leave it behind her and fulfill her duties as an army wife with the best effort she could. When they had been married for about three months, orders came that the regiment was moving west to another post. She was advised that she couldn't take her possessions with her; only what was necessary for their daily needs. Sadly, she sent a note for her father to store the items in his attic, and he sent a wagon and driver to take them away.

Summer found them at Fort Leavenworth. The post was large, with long, multistoried barracks faced with long porches. Green, branching trees dotted the landscape, although the broad, cleared expanses were as likely to be muddy pits as covered in grass. A prison was under construction, being built of stone and brick, with high-pitched roofs and towers at each corner. Their married quarters were improved over their original honeymoon suite, with three full rooms and an indoor latrine for their private use. Three fireplaces kept them warm as toast, and one was retrofitted with a metal cook stove, making cooking a pleasure. Running water came from an overhead cistern, and Becca discovered a tin bathing tub that she shared with two other couples. She had funds to hire a maid two days a week, for cleaning and doing of the laundry, and the young married couple had many opportunities for making friendships and a pleasant social life.

Even so, time passed slowly for the pair as they tried to make the best of the situation. The captain remained aloof from Becca when not called upon to engage her in friendly conversation. He spent many hours at the officers' club, doing what, she couldn't say.

— 4 —

Captain William Lankford sat proudly on his steed, the morning breeze yet to rise and the air still and damp in the dawn. He touched the animal on its flanks with one heel, and the beast moved forward, leading his company of Cavalry out of the fort. The eastern sky retained the faintest of pink on the horizon. The dust and manure of the parade ground irritated his eyes, and he attempted to blink the grittiness away. He turned in the saddle to see his sergeant, Fleming Barker, slightly behind him, and a private, Kimberly, he thought, carrying the company banner. It was a familiar scene for him, having ridden out of one post or another since he'd first joined the Army. A new post, a new commanding officer, but what wasn't familiar on this morning was his half-hearted attempt to assure his wife of his safety during the patrol.

He remembered their first morning of married

bliss. He'd simply left, without a word of affection or encouragement. He'd learned since to be sociable, at least. She tried to hide her fears, but he knew she worried for him.

His wife! He sighed. How had he managed to get himself into this situation? He'd never meant to marry, certainly not to a dashing woman like Rebecca Rains. It seemed in the last few weeks, they'd been to one party after another. He hated the socials at the post, preferring to be riding as he was now with his troopers. He tried to remember who it was that had told him Becca Rains was a loose woman. Ah, Tom Stoner, that was who; the assistant quartermaster. Lieutenant Stoner had been left behind when his orders came to report to Fort Leavenworth. It was a good thing, because it was hard to control his emotions around the man, whom he'd thought to be his friend.

He'd not been interested at first in the gossip among the officers that night, but he was already slightly disgruntled by the letter that had arrived from his brother. Jacob had married Jennie Carpenter, the only woman whom he'd been drawn to during his recent leave home to see his family. With Jennie now out of his reach, he'd thought to entertain himself with the lovely Becca, but instead woke up the next morning in a tangle from which he couldn't extract himself without causing a scandal. His military career was too important to become engaged in a battle with her father over the night's dalliance. He'd heard the rumors about her pregnancy and knew that the father of her child couldn't be him. The marriage, however, was inevitable, so he settled his mind and married her anyway. The matter rankled, still, leaving him angry and resentful that he'd fallen into her matrimonial trap.

It was clear that the rumors and the insinuations were unfounded, as he found out himself on his wedding night. It'd been a shock to discover his bride a virgin. He could still feel the relief and the surprise. He'd been fully prepared to accept his part in the drama at Gladys Kitchum's ball, but was still trying to cope with the thought that he might be forced to accept another man's child as his own when he left his future father-in-law's presence. He knew from the frowns and quiet looks of the other officers when he'd returned to base and told the Colonel of his approaching marriage that they were counting the days and weeks until she delivered. The move to Fort Leavenworth saved him from that humiliation.

His attention was caught by a movement to the left, and he saw that the colonel had ridden away from the front of the column, formed by a long caravan heading west. The whole group stretched out maybe a mile, what with the colonel and the engineers, including Brinkley; Captain Lankford's Cavalry; Lieutenant Jones' Infantry; Lieutenant Preston's two cannons; two supply wagons; one hospital wagon; plus several loose horses and the Indian scouts. At the present, Preston brought up the rear, since the weapons riding on caissons and pulled by mules were heavy and ponderous.

He brought his attention to his business and cast an eye at his sergeant. Barker was looking at the colonel with suspicion and turned to look back at the long line of horsemen. Lankford trusted Barker completely. If something was going on, he was the one to know. The colonel signaled for the men to stop, and Lankford raised his hand for his men to obey the signal. The column came to a halt, while the horses blew the dust from their nostrils, and the creak of saddle leather and jangling of swords and stirrups broke the silence of the morning. The sun was now higher in the sky and felt warm on his back. Several of the men shifted to a more comfortable position in their saddles. Lankford would have loved to walk a while but didn't dare move from his seat.

"Lankford." A loud call came from the commanding officer.

Lankford kicked his horse to get him to move forward. He let his body shift smoothly from side to side, his saber clanking softly, and his animal's feet stirring dust as he moved. He drew his reins beside the colonel, stopping his beast.

"Yes, Sir. What seems to be the trouble?"

The colonel turned and looked forward, then back at his men. "The scouts haven't come back from their reconnaissance of the area around the butte. Take a couple of men and see if you can observe anything out of the ordinary, like dust on the horizon or smoke signals. Try not to draw attention to yourself. Come back and report to me. Don't alarm the men. We'll take a short breather and rest the horses."

Lankford had been so engrossed in his thoughts that he hadn't realized the absence of the Indian scouts. He signaled for Sergeant Barker and Private Venable to follow him and started his horse at a trot toward the butte, his eyes open to the danger. He took one short look behind him to his men, and saw them dismounting from their horses. Barker shouted and pointed to the butte.

The Ute scouts, bareback and with quivers of arrows strapped to their horses' sides, were racing back to the column, their horses seeming to fly through the grass, kicking up dust as they ran. Lankford could hear their yells on the wind and turned his horse, gave a signal to his companions and sprinted back to the colonel's side.

"The scouts have come across something," he said. "They're racing back from the butte."

The colonel wasted no time on further explanation, but gave the signal to mount and form a defensive position. Lankford led his company into their usual formation on the front flank and awaited the arrival of the scouts. Immediately behind the scouts, about halfway to the ridge, he could see about one hundred Indians with unpainted faces, shouting and waving lances and rifles in the air.

The scouts approached the colonel, gave their

guttural explanation of what was happening and passed down the line of skirmish and out of sight of Lankford, who was surprised to see the Indians suddenly stop and gather around their war chief. He sat tall on his beast, his headdress of eagle feathers running down his back. His stitched and embroidered leggings revealed bare feet and calves.

Lankford remained tense, waiting for the sound of gunfire or orders to retreat.

Unexpectedly, the Indian chief let out a guttural cry, and the troupe of savages turned their horses and galloped back toward the butte. The colonel called for his officers to attend him, and Lankford; Jones, commander of Company C; Preston, commanding the light artillery; and Brinkley of Company E of the Engineering Squad, nudged their horses close to the man.

"The scouts say that this group has a camp near the butte. They don't seem hostile; they have their women and children with them. There are about one hundred horses, some cattle and dogs guarded by a few men on horseback. The women seem to be working with fresh meat. White Bear says they've been hunting buffalo and seemed to be as startled to see us, as we are to see them. He suggests we circle around them and head in a more easterly direction. That's what we'll do. Captain Lankford, leave about a half dozen men behind to watch for trouble. If the Indians don't follow us; we'll keep going east, then turn north again. Be cautious, men; it could be a trick. Stay close in formation and alert for signs of trouble." The colonel turned his horse and moved back to his usual place at the head of the column.

Lankford explained the situation to Sergeant Barker, who relayed the instructions to his men, and the column started again, heading in an easterly line. After noon, they moved directly north to northwest until sundown. It was a long day's march, and after camping overnight along a deep ravine, they arrived the next day at Fort Riley, where Lieutenant Preston's light artillery, along with the colonel and Lieutenant Jones' Infantry troops, would remain, along with one of the supply wagons, and the hospital wagon with Doctor McKinsey and his two assistants. Captain Brinkley's men formed an engineering group and would set out to map the U.S. border with Canada, from the Dakotas westward.

Captain Lankford and his troopers remained at Fort Riley for four days, enjoying the sometimes raucous hospitality of the traders and buffalo hunters. There was liquor, homemade and otherwise, shooting games, rabbit skinning contests, and one night, several Indian women to entertain. During daylight hours, Lankford, Lieutenant Preston and some of the men scouted the area, and agreed that it would someday become a fine place for an industrious farmer or rancher to build a home.

On the fifth day, before dawn, they started the long trek back to Fort Leavenworth. As the highest-ranking officer, Captain Lankford felt the weight of heavy responsibility on his shoulders. He led his own company, with Sergeant Barker, and with Corporal Andrew Fortune and Private Belvedere Jackson acting as scouts. They were followed by the supply wagon, driven by the cook and muleskinner, Amos Fielding. Next came two wagons of settlers who were set on traveling east to Missouri, about twenty head of cattle, some sheep and two dozen loose horses; and bringing up the rear guard was Lieutenant Macklin with Company F. Private Venable would act as his messenger between the two companies of Cavalry. He disapproved of the civilians traveling with them, but agreed with Lieutenant Macklin that they couldn't travel through Indian country alone.

He had met with the men and women of the wagons the night before. Hezekiah Hawkins and his wife's brother, James Atkinson, had tried farming in the Colorado Territory for three years, and didn't like it. Hezekiah had developed a persistent cough from the high altitude and the cold, which they hoped would improve upon their return. They, their wives and children were headed back to Indiana, where they each had large families, but would first have to cross the Missouri River near Fort Leavenworth. They agreed that Colorado was good farming country, with lots of timber and opportunity for a growing family, but it was too lonely and isolated for them. The Hawkins family consisted of four small children, and Ruth

Atkinson had three boys.

Hezekiah Hawkins was a large, aggressive man, with a loud voice and crude manners, and his wife, Mattie, seemed timid and worn down with the labor of housekeeping and raising children. James Atkinson was average in height with a dark beard and stooped shoulders. He'd come west with his sister's husband four years before because of the long drought and ruined crops of his farm. He'd left it with his younger brother to work the fields, when the group headed west with a wagon train. His wife, Ruth, was a comely woman, with blonde hair and blue eyes. She had a good sense of humor, and kept her brood of children quiet with a firm hand. Lankford got the impression that he was going east under protest and would have become prosperous in Colorado, if not for the dominant influence of his brother-in-law. But, it wasn't his business. His duty was to see them safely escorted to the fort where they would find another means of transportation to their destination.

Captain Lankford sat on a large bay horse and rode ahead to consult with his scouts. They were near the butte area where they had previously encountered the Indian encampment, and he sent Fortune and Jackson to investigate the situation. He rode back to the side of the sergeant and found Ruth Atkinson riding beside him.

"Good day, Mrs. Atkinson, I see you're feeling fine today. Although I wouldn't like to dampen your enthusiasm for riding, it would be best if you remain near your wagon for the next few hours. Sergeant Barker, please escort the lady back to her husband."

It was clearly a dismissal, but the lady didn't acquiesce willingly. "Captain, it's such a lovely, clear day, and riding in the wagon grows tiresome. I see no danger in my riding with the soldiers." She tossed her head, and one long blonde curl bounced on her shoulder. She flashed her blue eyes at him and smiled.

He wasn't impressed.

"Ma'am, sometimes the danger isn't seen until it's upon us. There's an Indian camp near the butte over there, and if they decide to raid our party for fresh horses or the cattle, you might think about the health of your boys before your own pleasure." He gave her a piercing stare, and she turned her horse and rode away, the sergeant following at a slower pace.

Lankford knew he'd made an enemy of the woman, and it might cost him dearly later, but for now, he had to think of the whole party, not the spite of a foolish woman. He told Private Venable to tell the men guarding the horses and cattle to be on the alert for trouble and sent him to tell Fielding, driving the supply wagon, to prepare if necessary for an attack. He told him to tell Lieutenant Macklin to bring his men closer to the front as protection for the wagons and settlers and the animals. He gazed over his long column and saw that his orders were obeyed.

The afternoon shadows lengthened, and he began to think he was overly cautious, when a loud shout was heard and the two scouts were seen flying over the ridge. Lankford gave the signal to his men, and as they prepared for battle, his men grouped into a circle, with the wagons and loose horses and cattle in the center, and dismounted from their horses. Corporal Fortune alighted in a cloud of dust and reported that there were about twenty Indians on horseback heading toward them, with their faces painted and lances and weapons ready for battle.

Lankford remained on his bay horse waiting where his men and the settlers could see him. The situation was tense, but not especially alarming, as they waited. He could see the children milling about the wagons and wished he could notify the men to lift them inside, but he couldn't risk Venable on the errand; he needed him in case he should have to send him to Lieutenant Macklin. Now, he could see the dust of those twenty horses coming over the ridge, and suddenly, he heard the loud shouts of Indians.

Several of the settlers began screaming, and with their high-pitched voices, he assumed it was the women. The men grabbed children by the waist and helped them clamber into the wagons. Finally, he thought, they do something right. As the savages grew closer, gunfire erupted from the line of Indians, and arrows flew through the air, with several piercing the wagons' canvas tops. A trooper fell to the dirt, holding his injured leg. Lankford's men lifted their weapons in preparation to return fire.

The skirmish was short and loud, and only two men were injured: one private shot in the arm; another in the leg. One horse was brought down, but the rest were safe. Lankford supposed they were only after the horses and cattle, or supplies in the wagon, but the defense was too strong. They rode away after about an hour, taking their dead and wounded with them, and headed back to the butte area. Lankford saw that his wounded were taken care of and ordered the men to put some distance between them. The column rode out in its original order, but with Lieutenant Macklin's company spread out in a v-shaped column as a rear guard.

Hezekiah Hawkins came up and rode beside Lankford for a while before he was able to speak.

"Captain, I thank you for your protection of my family and animals, but I must protest the harsh treatment of my sister-in-law before the battle. She's a gently reared woman and not accustomed to being ordered about by men like you. She's been riding since her youth and is capable of making her own decisions regarding her behavior. I shall report this incident to your commanding officer when we arrive at Fort Leavenworth." He huffed and spat tobacco juice on the ground.

"Thank you, Hawkins, but I shall use whatever

tactics I need to use to keep this column safe until we reach the fort. By all means, report my conduct to the commanding officer, if you wish. But, I would suggest that Mrs. Atkinson or your good wife not ride in the open and to keep the children close to the wagons for the rest of the journey." He continued to ride as before, and Hawkins slowly rode back to his family. Lankford was troubled but didn't let his emotions show before his troops.

They camped that night with extra guards, expecting the Indians to sneak up in the darkness, but no sound or sight of them occurred. The next morning, Lankford relaxed and the men began to sing or whistle as they rode along. He noticed that the women didn't stray from the wagons, but walked sedately with the children near them. The rovers kept the cattle and sheep tightly bunched and the horses double guarded, for they were the most valuable commodity to the Indians. Their travelling day ended at sunset, and tents were set up and campfires lit. Sergeant Fleming Barker took out his old guitar and sang a sad, lonely song of lost love, and the men lounged around the fires as usual.

A week of slow travel found the column near Fort Leavenworth. The scenery had changed from sandy desert and protruding rocks to scraggly trees and green grass. The long, purple-gray lines of mountain ridges were behind them in the west. They stayed far from the river, but not so far that they couldn't lead the animals in groups to drink and carry pails for their cooking fires. The trees gave cooling shade, and the twittering of birds was a calming accompaniment at sunset as they settled in the limbs of the willows and reeds along the banks.

Lankford checked on the wounded men and found that their injuries were almost healed. He was grateful for the attention of Sergeant Barker and his tender concern for his men. Barker could be an intimidating man when giving orders, but he saw that his men and animals were well cared for. The men, in most cases, looked to him for leadership. He'd been in the Army for over twenty years and had fought against the Indians many times. Lankford took the time to thank him for his service during the trip.

The high walls of the fort seemed strangely foreign as the column approached. The surrounding area was covered with trees and animals, and seemingly hundreds of men in uniform and on horseback roamed the grounds. Shacks and tents were erected to accommodate the merchants, visitors and troopers who didn't live inside the walls. The smell of cooking fires and burnt food filled the air with an alien scent. Corporal Fortune was sent ahead to give warning of their arrival; and the gates opened to receive the captain and his troops; leaving the wagons, horses, cattle and sheep outside with their guards until accommodations could be arranged for them. Hawkins, Atkinson and their families felt it their privilege to accompany Captain Lankford, and he didn't object to their presence. He motioned for them to park their wagons near the settlement of villagers.

He reported to the commanding officer and was told to write his report and dismiss his men, after seeing they were taken care of. He left the office with a feeling of deep relief and headed to his quarters. His heart was banging like a drum in his ribs, for he hadn't seen his wife in over a month. He was hot, tired and sweating, but there was no time or opportunity to clean, shave or change clothes before he saw her standing at the door of his rooms. He walked across the parade ground toward her. Out of the corner of his eye, he saw a glance of shock from Ruth Atkinson. He ignored her. She probably thought him a rude officer who had no interest in women, either that, or no woman would desire him. Here he was approaching his beautiful wife, and the woman could watch or not, as she chose.

He took Becca into his arms for a hug, but she drew back after a while and laughed. She wrinkled her nose at the smell. He grabbed her again and kissed her long on the lips. He could smell the faint scent of rose water in her hair, his favorite fragrance.

"Oh, Darling, it's good to see you. Go take care of your men, and I'll draw water for a bath and set out clean clothes for you. Will we eat here or in the officers' quarters tonight? I have some beans and a fresh loaf of bread for your supper."

"I'm sorry you've worked so hard, but I can't stay to enjoy it. We've brought along some settlers and their wives and children, so I suppose the major will want us to eat at the long table tonight. I'll let you know as soon as we see to our horses and tackle. You look beautiful. Are you well?" Lankford studied Becca's face as she laughed again. He knew that she enjoyed the rituals at the commandant's table, but he hated it, and especially tonight, when he desired to be alone with her.

After the weeks on the trail, the fort seemed safe and peaceful to Captain Lankford. A bird fluttered in a tree, and after a moment, it whistled a jaunty tune. He kissed his wife on the cheek, reassuring her he would return, and to have his bath ready. He strode off with a new confidence and felt even the officers' table wouldn't be too much to endure for his wife's company.

Lankford returned several hours later, having settled his charges, tired, but ready for a meal. He gave Becca the news she hoped for, that they would be dining with the officers and their visitors. A bath, a shave and clean clothes were just what he needed. He was his most charming, for he found the company of the woman to whom he was married preferable to those who had shared his travels the past month. He felt his eyes were opened for the first time in their marriage, as if he was seeing Becca fresh and new.

The meal was a formal affair at the beginning.

The unfamiliar guests made for awkward conversation, but the barriers began to fall, and more ribald conversation took sway. The Atkinsons seemed miffed at the turn of jokes and teasing among the Army fellows, but they were glad to be back in camp, and the company and food were good. Lankford laughed riotously at a story from his wife, and in front of God and everybody, he kissed her on the forehead, bringing nods of approval from the officers around him.

After the meal concluded, Captain William Lankford and his wife, Rebecca, walked across the parade ground to their quarters. It had started out a long, dreadful ordeal, sitting at the major's table, trying his best to be hospitable to his fellow officers and the civilians that gathered around the table, then things had shifted for him. Becca was at her best, and he secretly noticed that Ruth Atkinson bristled at the sight and sound of his lively wife, dressed in a teal wool frock with gold braided trim at the edge of her skirt, her pearls gleaming in the candlelight against her white Garibaldi blouse, entertaining with such grace and charm. She was jealous, he was certain. Well, his duty was discharged, and he was free for the night. He could relax, enjoy the company of his wife and listen to her tales of duty while he'd been away. He enjoyed the sound of her voice and her laugh, more than he cared to admit. The memories of those first few days together came back in a flood, and he took her arm to hurry her along.

— 5 —

As the couple made their way from the officers' celebration, Becca was grateful for William's hand on her arm, for she was weary, more so than she might have expected. She supposed she'd grown used to eating alone and not forcing joviality where there was none. She enjoyed the entertainment, but as strongly, she'd sensed the hostility of the pretty settler who had sat across from her and William. The woman gave him darting, hostile glances, then laughed and tried to get the attention of Lieutenant Macklin sitting beside her. Becca had never felt jealousy before, and she was disconcerted to think that she was capable of the emotion.

She shivered in the brisk night air, and she pulled her shawl tighter. She was pleased when William wrapped his arms across her shoulders and held her to him.

William opened the door and walked into the

room after his wife. He struck a match and lighted a candle as Becca lifted her shawl from her shoulders and spread it across the horsehair chair that served as their only true luxury item in the quarters. The room was mostly stark and bare, with shelves across one wall with books that had been read repeatedly while her husband had been away. The fireplace was dark. The large bed seen through the door across from them covered most of the floor space in the small room, and in the third room, a simple table and two ladderback chairs sat beside the metal cook stove. He lighted an oil lamp, giving the room greater light, and heaved a sigh as he unbuttoned his coat and drew it from his shoulders.

"God, I'm tired. I thought the dinner would never end. You looked lovely tonight, Becca. I was quite proud to claim you as my own possession among all the women." He sat on the edge of the chair to draw off his dress boots and looked up in surprise at her reaction.

"I'm not your possession, William. Why do you say such things? I'm your lawful wife, not some slave that you bought at auction." Becca blew out her checks and frowned at him. "And, who is that Ruth Atkinson? I thought she was going to eat you for dinner. She kept looking at you with such admiration. Did you have an affair with her while you were gone?" A month! A month he'd been on the trail with her and those filthy people. No wonder he left her alone during his scouting expeditions. He probably had Indian women out there, too, for trysts in the dark of the night. After the trying evening, she'd wanted their night to be one of warmth and welcoming, and now he'd irritated her. She turned from him, wrapping her arms around herself, and wished she were back in her mother's house, with servants, vast green lawns, and fine clothes to wear every day.

"What? An affair with Mrs. Atkinson? How can you accuse me of this, when she was accompanied at all times with her husband and three children, while I was busy with my duties as commander of the Cavalry? When would I have had time to dally with a foolish, self-centered woman?" William stood, walking to stand directly behind her, and he grasped her by the shoulders. "I've missed you, my wife, and after spending the month with those frightful women, I've wanted nothing else than to come back to you. There's been no affair. You must trust me in this."

Becca started to cry. She knew she was being foolish, but she couldn't help it. The excitement of the day after the long period of loneliness was overwhelming. She hiccupped. She drew a handkerchief from the pocket of her dress and wiped her eyes.

"I'm sorry. I know you wouldn't do that, but I was so angry when I saw the way she looked at you. I was jealous." She turned to him, looking him in the eyes, her tears running down her hot cheeks. "God help me, for the first time in my life

I was jealous that another woman was paying attention to you."

William took the handkerchief from her hand and wiped her eyes. He kissed her gently on the cheek.

"I'm the one who's sorry. Of course, you're not my possession, my dear wife, although, I consider you my responsibility and my friend. It wasn't affection that you saw in the eyes of Ruth Atkinson, my dear; it was hatred, or something like it. You see, twice I was required to correct her on the trip. She was apt to wander astray on her horse, ignoring the danger to herself and the men. Hawkins said he would report me to my commanding officer, and I suppose I'll have to appear before him tomorrow to be reprimanded. But, I couldn't let her just ride off on her own, away from the wagons and troops, you see. I had to send Private Venable after her the second time. The first time, I caught her flirting with Sergeant Barker, and you know he's a droll fellow. Now, love, dry your eyes and think no more about the silly woman. I'm home now for a while, at least, and we must make the best of the short time we have before I must ride away again. Don't let us spoil our precious time together in quarrels."

He was so humble and charming that Becca couldn't hold out longer. She slid her arms around him, and laughing, they fell to the floor, entwined in each other's arms. It was a long time before he blew out the lights and crawled into bed. Becca held William tightly, whispering that the floor wasn't the best place in which to make love to his wife on his first night together after a month away, but it was satisfying.

****

Becca rose the next morning, all smiles, and laid out a small fire in the cook stove. After a time, the room began to warm, and she set out a skillet to warm. Unwrapping a slab of cured bacon, she cut a half-dozen slices and placed them in the pan to cook, also for grease for the eggs. A pot of coffee was next. She returned several times to the bedroom to glance at the bed, thrilled at the lump lying under the quilts. He was home. It seemed so unbelievable. He would soon rise and eat and go outside to his duties as commander of a company of Cavalry, but for this blessed moment, he was her man. She hummed under her breath.

William called, "I hear humming; is that bacon I smell?"

"And coffee," Becca returned, smiling.

"I'm torn, my love, between my desire to bring you back to bed, or to rise and start the day. It's a shame my duty to my occupation and my men is so strong." She appeared at the door and watched him stretch and rise from the bed. He walked across the room, unclothed, and hugged her. She laughed, telling him her bacon would soon burn. He did want to eat, didn't he? He let her go, looking through his uniforms for the daily set he would wear for regular maneuvers.

"Good morning to you, too, my dear," he teased, with a glance to her occasionally, as he pulled his clothing on. "That smells delicious. I sometimes wish that I wasn't in the Army; so you could have your own full kitchen and oil cooking range. Would you like that?" He pulled on his pants and buttoned the fly, and reached for his shirt.

"That would be nice; but you'd never leave the Army, would you? It's your career, what you've done all your adult life." Becca took the bacon from the skillet and placed it on a plate. She drew the dinnerware from a drawer under the counter top in the old cabinet and set the table. She broke four eggs in the grease to let them cook.

"I suppose you're right. I couldn't give up my career for now, not with hostilities building in the eastern states. Maybe in a few years when all is quiet again, we can discuss the matter once more. The settlers, Hawkins and Atkinson, have been farming in Colorado, and have said good things about the soil and the huge forests and wide rivers." He paused and wrinkled his brow. "I'd like to see the Pacific Ocean. Maybe, we could go to Oregon. I'm not sure I'd like farming, but there must be something I could do to make a living." He sat down and poured a cup of coffee and took a small sip.

"Bacon, too? It's hot, yet." Becca held out a

plate with the slices cooling on a cloth. Her heart warmed at his words. She'd never heard him speak of a future for them that didn't include his military appointments. He picked up a piece of bacon and ate it, and Becca felt her attachment to the man at her side growing deeper by the mouthful. She cut several thick slices off a loaf of bread. Lifting the eggs to a plate, and draining some of the grease away, she toasted the bread in the skillet, turning it once until it was golden brown on both sides.

"It's good, wife. You've learned to cook very well." He smiled. "What do you think of Oregon?"

"Oregon? But, surely, we couldn't go to Oregon. Why not live in Missouri, across the river? I've heard the women say it's good farm land. Several of the men have bought farms after their retirement from the army life." Becca was thinking of her father's home. She grew up a merchant's daughter; she hadn't thought she would live any other life, until she met William Lankford.

"Missouri, huh?" William sat quietly eating his food. "You know, my love, I've been thinking of the settlers and their families. They'd been to Colorado and taken out claims on the free land, but were dissatisfied. Would we become bored and dissatisfied with a farmer's life as well? I don't know. I wanted to be a soldier since childhood, was even educated on the duties and responsibilities of an army life from a youth. I can't imagine another way of life for myself. You think I could become a farmer?"

Becca pondered his question for a moment, as she sat down at her own meal. She took a sip of coffee. She knew what he hadn't said. He'd never wanted a wife, either, and the responsibility of children. Yet, last night and today had been different. William had been different. For the first time, she felt like he really loved her.

"Maybe, Captain Lankford," she offered with a flirtatious smile, dropping her lashes over her misting eyes. "I'd be willing to give it a try if you ever think it's something we can do."

He smiled as he finished his meal and rose, put his hat on his head and went out the door, whistling.

Becca, left alone in the room, cleared the table. She poured some hot water from the kettle into a pan and placed it back in the coals of the fireplace. As she washed the dishes, she thought of what William had said. Did she want to live on a farm? Would she be content as a sheltered woman; never to hear of the danger of war and the sound of the bugle's loud wail early in the morning; to see the Stars and Stripes flapping in the breeze; nor watch the men marching in cadence on the parade ground? No. She enjoyed the excitement; the tingle of danger; the gossip of the other officers' wives; the sight of uniforms with shining buckles, marching feet, and the clatter of swords and the boom of the guns. The few months she'd spent on the Army post was her life now; and she was reluctant to go back to the days of yore, to the chores of her youth. She would tell him when he came home at noon.

She was thwarted in her desire to share with her husband about her excitement and newfound enjoyment of army life; for he rushed back just before noon to say he'd been assigned to escort a caravan to Fort Gibson with supplies, rations and equipment for the western post. In the following week, his time was no longer his own to use as he pleased, as he gathered his straggling company together and mounted fresh horses before riding out again.

She watched as they lined up on the parade ground, and she waved as he rode through the gates of the post. She laughed as she turned away; he was home only one week and gone again. Well, that was the Army way; and she was content to have it so.

── Epilogue ──

William Lankford remained in the Army for another fifteen years before his retirement. He rose to the rank of Lieutenant Colonel and distinguished himself on the battlefield and the final post where he served as Post Commander. He was known for his integrity, his loyalty and sense of duty to his men and his country.

Through the years, the names and faces of the men who served under him blended into a long line of sergeants and privates and commissioned officers, and their wives and the civilians under his command. Becca followed him from post to post when she could; and remained behind to await his return when she couldn't. She became known for her courage, her grace and charm, whether at the dining table, or discharging a rifle from behind a barrier of wagons. They were married for fifty-two years. They had three children together: two sons and a daughter.

Lankford didn't become a farmer; choosing instead to live at Platte City, Missouri, across the river from Fort Leavenworth, and work as a carpenter. His fine furniture was sold in the family store purchased with money he'd saved through the years. He was given a gold pocket watch by his men, and he was known to take it out and gaze at the western horizon, as though waiting for the soldiers to return from their deployment. He lived to a ripe old age and was buried in the Fort Leavenworth cemetery with the highest honors.

Becca, who never again thought about her fine things stored long ago in her father's attic, followed him three years later and was buried beside him.

The Gold Nugget

— 1 —

Private First Class Malachi Clements wished he was dead.

He lay in the hospital bed listening to the groans and cries of the other patients around him, and the nightmare seemed endless. The pungent odor of human decay from the gangrene that seemed to invade every injury burned in his nose, stealing sleep from him. He took his right hand and felt again the bandage the doctors had placed around his left stub when they repaired the damage to his arm. It felt wet; damn, it was bleeding again. There was no odor, so he could hope he'd escaped the devil of gangrene. It didn't hurt so much now as it had at first; sometimes he even imagined he still had a hand there, and five fingers, as well. He glanced toward the end of the room and saw the light from the orderly's station. Should he call the man and tell him, or should he wait until daylight?

"Water." The voice from the bed next to him

came weakly and softly. "Mister, can you get me some water? My mouth is so dry."

Malachi was thirsty, too. He managed to sit up but felt dizzy, so remained on the side of the bed for a few minutes, regaining his strength. An odor of stale urine came from across the room, someone unable to hold his water, and unable to make his way to the latrine. It was strong enough that the mattress must be soaked. He took a step on the floor, and it seemed like a thousand needles jabbed his feet at once. It was the first time he'd stood since the horrible afternoon a week ago when shrapnel from Rebel artillery fire had severed his hand, shredding his flesh into a wasted lump. He took a step and then another. I can do this, he told himself. I can!

He slowly reached the table between the beds and poured the precious, clear fluid into a glass. First, he selfishly quenched his own thirst; then poured some more for his mate. He held it to the man's mouth while he drank. The prone man took a sip and coughed. Malachi had to draw back to keep from being sprayed by the mix of water and saliva. He put the glass to the patient's parched lips a second time, and the man drank a bit more and motioned that he'd had enough.

Malachi started back to his bed.

"Thanks, Yank. Can you spare a smoke? Haven't had a good smoke in a month." The man's voice seemed stronger.

The doctor had told the man that he shouldn't

smoke, but Malachi knew how it felt. He hadn't had a smoke since he joined the Union army and was sent to camp for training.

"Sorry, old man, but I don't have any. I'd like to have one myself," Malachi whispered, with his mouth close to the man's ear, so they wouldn't draw the attention of the sleepers nearby.

"Don't matter anyway, I suppose. I won't last another day in this place. What's your name, Yank? Mine's Private Jethro Belton from Alabama. Wish I'd stayed there."

Malachi was startled, both because of the man's acceptance of his impending death and because he was from the South. This was a United States Army Hospital. He didn't know the Army took in Southern men. He must be a prisoner of war. Malachi moved across the foot of space that separated the beds to his own and sat to think this through a minute. He leaned over to the other man and whispered to him.

"My name's Malachi Clements from Illinois." He laughed bitterly. "I'm a silversmith by trade, but don't guess I'll be doing that again with one hand. What are you in for? Were you at Chickamauga?"

Belton coughed again. "I don't have much time to discuss the details of the war, Clements. Look in that pouch in the toe of my boot, if you can find it."

In the semi-darkness, Malachi could see the pair of ragged boots under the man's bed and put his hand in and brought out a cloth pouch about the size of his thumb, tied with a string of leather. He handed it to Belton.

"No, you take it. Hide it! These doctors will steal it for themselves." The man coughed roughly, then drew a ragged breath, the air wheezing in and out of his mouth. "Lean closer and listen. Got that little pebble up near Pike's Peak in '62 and thought I'd get back there after the war, but I won't make it. You take it and the map and help yourself to what you find there."

The man lay back, exhausted, and coughed again until Malachi grew worried. The poor soul eventually calmed down and seemed to be asleep. Malachi crawled into his bed, the pouch in his hand. What did it mean? He saw the orderly start walking down the path between the beds, carrying the lantern. His uniform, that of a private with a green half-chevron on the left forearm, rustled softly as he walked. The light in his hand was a dim glow, creating shifting, shadowed corners that moved as he walked. He must have heard them whispering and come to find out what was going on. Malachi closed his hand over the pouch and covered his head with the scratchy brown blanket. He pretended to be asleep. He could see the light of the lantern through his closed lids and tried not to blink.

After a minute or two, the man moved on. He shined the light in the face of the man next to Malachi and must have been satisfied, for he continued down the row of cots. Malachi heard him whispering to another man and hoped the fellow hadn't told him what he'd heard, if he'd heard anything. The orderly completed the row and started up the opposite side of the room. Malachi watched from his pillow. When the man was settled again, hunched over some papers on his desk, Malachi drew out the pouch and looked inside.

Gold! He would swear that the tiny object was a piece of gold about the size of a bean. There was a folded section of paper in the pouch, but Malachi was afraid to open it, in case it crinkled in the silence of the room. He decided to wait until daylight to see what it said. He closed his eyes and wondered about the man in the bed. Why would he give the pouch to him, a stranger? And, a Union Army soldier, besides. Pushing the questions away as best he could, he accepted he must be patient and wait until morning to ask him. Several times, Malachi glanced at the bed next to him, but the man didn't stir. He slipped the miniature pouch under his pillow and kept his hand on it in the dark.

A noise at the end of the room woke Malachi from a sound sleep, in which he dreamed of tramping through the woods, the loud yells of the enemy on both sides of him. He looked up at the dingy flypaper strips hanging from the ceiling and realized that he was still in the hospital. He grasped the pouch in his hand and felt the solid stone inside. He must find a place to hide it before the doctor came to look at his bandage. Malachi had forgotten that the bandage had felt damp in the night. He managed to sit up and cautiously made his way to the outhouse in back.

In the dim light of the latrine, shadows danced in a ghostly haze, and he opened the pouch and looked at the nugget again. It wasn't shiny like polished gold, more like a dull yellow piece of dirt, but he could tell it wasn't a common clod of hard clay. He opened the paper to find a quitclaim deed to a property in Colorado Territory with a small map drawn at the bottom. He wasn't familiar with the mountains, but he remembered reading about the discovery of gold at Pike's Peak before the war. The sound of footsteps approached, and he quickly folded the paper, put it and the nugget in the pouch and closed his hand around it. As he moved out of the building, he glanced at his left sleeve and saw the bright red stain. No chance of hiding the pouch in the bandage. He walked back to the door and made his way slowly to his bed.

Malachi's trip outside left him exhausted; his heart beat fast, and his breath was shallow. He couldn't quit thinking about what he held in his hand. Gold could make him rich, if he could find enough. He hoped the doctor didn't notice his excitement, and he forced himself to calm down, once again putting the pouch under his pillow and praying that no one would find it.

Once the room lightened with the morning, the doctor arrived and began making his rounds. He was a tall man, wearing a long apron, blood-stained in several places. Coming to Malachi, he called to the orderly that the bandage on his arm needed changing. They pulled the damp and bloody strips of cloth away, setting them in an enameled pan for disposal, and rewrapped the arm. The process was excruciating, leaving Malachi panting with pain, and with sweat soaking his nightshirt.

Once they went on their way, Malachi tore his eyes from the whitewashed ceiling and felt for the pouch. Don't let the doctors get it, Belton had said. Malachi found a small slit in the bandage, and with his finger, broadened it enough to put the pouch inside. He made sure nothing was showing. He turned his head to speak to Belton, to tell him where he'd hidden the pouch, to find a different patient, a man with red hair and a scraggly beard. Where was Belton, with his black hair? He glanced under the bed to find the man's boots gone. With a cold shudder of realization, he suspected the Angel of Death had passed down this very room during the long, black night, and he would never speak with the Southern soldier again.

Breakfast was brought on a gurney, the worn wheels clattering on the wooden floor; and the sound of men's groaning and the rattling of trays and dishes distracted him for a moment. Malachi made the effort to sit up when the bulky orderly, who looked to be chosen for the job for his size and ability to hold screaming patients during painful medical procedures, placed a tray with breakfast meats and other items on the side of his bed; beside him stood a woman. He blinked at the sight.

"I see you're awake, Mr. Clements. That's good. Do you remember me from yesterday, Mrs. Phillips? I'm a civilian, trained to help with medical duties. I'm here to make sure you get a good breakfast to build up your strength. Do you need help with your meat?" The short, plump woman wearing a white dress was gray-haired and friendly. She didn't wait for an answer but took the knife and fork and proceeded to cut one of the slices of meat into bite-size pieces, commenting on what a lovely, sunny day it looked to be.

What good was a sunny day to a man too weak to stand on his feet for more than fifteen minutes? he wanted to retort. He hated the thought that he couldn't cut his own ham, but he was aware that she had pretty, brown eyes. She poured him a cup of coffee and started to move to the next bed on his left, followed by the orderly.

"Mrs. Phillips, what happened to the man in the bed next to me?" Malachi held his breath for the answer. He nodded his head toward the sleeping, red-haired man.

"Oh," she glanced that direction and put her hand to her mouth for a moment, "I believe they moved Mr. Belton to another room." She scurried away with the burly man pushing the heavy gurney.

Damn you, Angel of Death, he thought. As for the nurse, either she had intentionally lied, or she didn't know. He supposed that when a man died, they didn't want to alarm the other patients, else they panic and cause trouble.

With his good hand, clumsily, he ate his breakfast, as much as he could stomach, and pushed the tray away, careful not to spill any leftover food on the bed. He lay back on his pillow; his mind going over the events of the night. He felt guilty for some reason; he should turn the pouch over to the authorities, maybe. As he lay there, his mind drifted back to the thoughts that had occupied him in the last week since he woke up with one hand. He remembered the golden-haired girl who had danced with him in the spring before he was drafted into the Army. Roseanne was the prettiest girl he'd ever seen, with a dimple in her cheek and sky-blue eyes.

Malachi had received two letters from his brother, Elisha, while he was fighting in northern Virginia. One said that Roseanne had married a merchant in the town. At the time Malachi had grieved for a lost love, but now he thought it was as well that she'd married someone else. He had no plans to return to Springfield. His job as master silversmith was over and done. He couldn't handle with only five fingers the delicate tools and intricate pieces of metal for which he'd been trained.

However, he still had the knowledge that had been droned into his young brain about metals in general, and gold and silver, in particular. A dream began to build in his mind. If he could get on his feet and buy the necessary supplies, he'd make his way to Colorado Territory and see about that quitclaim deed. He began to figure how much it would take for a horse and pack mule, food and tools. A fly buzzed around the bandage on his arm, but it hadn't started bleeding. He watched the fly until it was caught on the sticky paper hanging from the ceiling. Just like me, he thought, caught tight and far from home. Tears of pity and anguish formed in his eyes, but he refused to let them fall.

— 2 —

Three weeks later, Private First Class Malachi Clements walked from the hospital, still somewhat shaky on his feet, but with money in his pocket and hope in his heart. His brother had dispatched a goodly sum for his care, which left him enough to buy a horse and saddle, if he was thrifty. He was mustered out and was free from all obligations to the United States Army because of his medical disability. He had the proper papers in his pocket if anyone challenged him, but he doubted if an officer would see his half arm and think him capable of holding a weapon.

However, Malachi, formerly of the U.S. Army, was set to prove them wrong.

The captain said that possibly, in time, there would be a pension for him, a certain amount set aside each month by the Congress for men like him. He didn't count on that happening. Captain Clarke offered to give the former soldier information on how to obtain a wooden arm with a hook for a hand, but Malachi turned that down flat. He wouldn't be treated like a freak and invalid, he told himself.

The first thing Malachi did was to find a restaurant and eat a substantial meal of sausage and gravy, with puffy, hot biscuits and yellow eggs, sunny side up. He went to a gunsmith and had a lightweight, modified rifle made with a shortened barrel, so he could carry and use it with one hand and his elbow stub.

While he waited for the alterations on the weapon, he visited several card games in the saloons. Whether from skill or luck, he most often came out with a large sum of money which he stuffed in a water-tight pouch in his lard can. He figured if a body wanted to rob him, he wouldn't think of messing up his hands in a tub of cooking grease.

Propping the barrel on his left elbow, and sighting along the round tube, he practiced for hours until he was an expert. He bought a small hand gun to carry in his left vest pocket. With the half-empty sleeve rolled up and tucked under, a person would be surprised to find that the former soldier could draw and shoot in an instant. He placed a long, thin knife in a leather scabbard in his boot top. A larger, heavier skinning knife rested in his pack.

He found the steamboat station and inquired of schedules to Colorado Territory. With a packet of pamphlets, maps and a colorful guide book, he rented a room for the week in a cheap but clean hotel. After an afternoon of reading and planning his trip, he decided to buy a new set of clothing, a sturdy pair of boots, and a heavy coat and rain slicker, but leave the rest of his needs until he reached St. Louis. He ignored the stares of the people on the sidewalk and the salesmen in the clothing store. The attendant who waited on him did give him a good tip on how to roll the empty sleeve and pin the unused part to his underarm with his right hand. Clean, freshly shaved and smelling of hair tonic, Malachi visited Madam Breaux's very exclusive gentlemen's establishment before he left his Army life behind him forever, the miniature pouch carefully hidden in a small secret pocket of his trousers.

If any of the visitors at Madam Breaux's establishment on that night met the same man six weeks later, they wouldn't have recognized him, for Malachi Clements was dressed in an entirely different disguise. His hair was longer, his full beard scraggly, his clothes worn and dusty from his long trek across the prairies, first on a steamboat to Jefferson City, then finding his way on coaches and by horseback towards the mountains. His horse, a blue roan, was valiant and strong; and his pack mule, whom he affectionately called Caesar, twitched his ears and nibbled at the dandelions growing along the sidewalks, as the trio started up the street to seek the real estate agent in Denver City in Colorado Territory.

The agent, dressed in a boiled white shirt and black frock coat, with stripped trousers, and sitting on a tall stool behind the counter, hardly looked at Malachi's empty sleeve. He introduced himself as Clarence Blevins. A short, dumpy fellow with sunken eyes and a red scar above his temple, his disinterested manner suggested he'd become accustomed to all kinds of men since the gold strike in 1861. When Malachi drew out the slip of paper with the quitclaim deed, he simply opened his large book and read what was on the page. He stood and went to the map on the wall, drew a line north from Denver City, muttered something under his breath and looked at the book again.

"I'm sorry, Mr. Clements, but that particular claim was declared abandoned about six months ago and given to a Mr. Potter from Indiana. There are three other claims open in the same section if you're interested in one of them." The harried clerk pushed his spectacles to the top of his head and squinted at the former United States soldier standing erect in front of him.

"Abandoned? How could it be declared abandoned? I have a legal paper saying it belongs to me, Malachi Clements." He'd carefully forged his own name to the deed after he found that Jethro Belton was indeed dead and buried, and hoped there was no one to challenge him at this end.

"The law says that if a claim isn't continuously worked for a period of one year, then it's considered abandoned. You look like a soldier; I suppose you didn't think the war was going to last so long. But, the law's the law. Would you like one of the other claims?" The agent, accustomed to dealing with frustrated miners, looked at Malachi to see what he decided to do about the situation, expecting him to continue his objections.

"How much for the other claims?" Malachi was adding the sum he had left in his pocket after buying the animals and supplies, wondering if he had enough.

"For all three?" The agent's voice squeaked with surprise. He brought his glasses down to his eyes and glanced at the book again. "Did I hear you right? You want all three claims?" He traced a line with his fingers and noticed that the three weren't connected to each other, but were on the same creek, about two hundred yards from top to bottom.

"Yes. All three claims. How much for all three?" Malachi watched the clerk and frowned, hoping the amount wasn't more than he had with him.

"It shows here that they aren't connected, having a claim between each of them. They're located on what the men are calling Fossil Creek, a tributary of the South Platte River; but I don't suppose that's its lawful name. There's a sort of trail or road along the side of the creek, but you'd have to go around the other two claims to get from one to the other. I can show you on the map, if you'd care to step around and see." The agent didn't wait for an answer. He was already looking at the giant board for himself. He traced his finger along the imaginary road and down to the first claim in question. Malachi duly watched the finger move up the large map. He saw only some squiggly lines and words on the paper.

"Here's the claim on your papers, now owned by Mr. Potter, and here's the first one of the abandoned claims. Between them is a Mr. Skinner, and here is the second about one hundred yards north and then the claim of Jude Barlow; and there's the upper one, near this clump of boulders and tall trees, from the drawn lines on the map." He left the map and drew another book from under his counter and turned pages until he found one he wanted. Malachi went back around the counter and stopped, leaning in to see the book.

"It says that the lower claim was abandoned by a Jed Brinkley, and that it has a cabin and shed on the property, with a sluice box and corrals. Mr. Brinkley, I remember, was one of the first to try mining along the creek. A friendly fellow, I believe he moved into Denver, but I couldn't say for sure, not knowing. He just up and moved out one day, leaving everything behind. Named the place Brinkley Manor, a fancy title to be sure." He looked up, but Malachi had no comment about a man he knew nothing about; he *was* interested in the fact that it had a cabin and corrals on the property.

"That claim, since it has a cabin already built,

would cost maybe twenty-five dollars in gold dust or government script." He received only a curt stare from the ex-soldier, so continued reading from the page.

"The middle claim was taken up by a Mr. Johnston of Illinois, but the cabin burned down last winter. He gave up and left for better diggings, he said. The land's for sale, but there's no shelter on it. It's described as near the high bank of a ridge and goes for about five miles into the forest. Since it hasn't been improved to any extent, it'll cost fifteen dollars." Once again he waited for an answer, but received none.

"Mr. Clements, I'm intrigued with your situation. Three claims, not connected to each other, would be hard to work by one man, and that with only one hand. Let me read the description of the third claim. It may be the very one you want. In my humble opinion, it's the best of the three."

He read the description of the last claim, sharing what he remembered of the man who'd made the original claim on the property: a tall broad-shouldered gentleman with a wife and passel of children, three boys, he remembered. The wife had gotten ill with the fever, and the man took his boys and moved to the city, leaving his claim abandoned. He had no idea what happened to the woman. Townsend, that was the man's name, he remembered at last. Jeffrey Townsend.

Malachi took a deep breath, remarking, "Not going to be the cheapest of the three, I suspect."

"As I said, the upper claim is the best in my opinion, but I have no reason to suppose that one claim's better than another. Gold is where you find it. I say that because it's only a few miles from the town of Astra, a hastily built squalor of tents, board-and-tar-paper shacks and gambling places; but at least supplies can be bought there if a man has the price. Huge boulders and tall trees, mostly pines, I understand, but a few firs and spruce, and chokeberry bushes. There's a cabin, but it's been empty for going on two years, so there's no telling if the roof's still on it. It gets the brunt of the snow storms in the winter, too. It'll cost you forty-two dollars." He took a pad and pencil and added up the amount. "That'll be eighty-seven dollars, with the additional filing fees and territorial taxes, of course. Say, ninety-two dollars, cash or a note for a monthly rate with interest, if you don't have the total. I get my share of the commission." He looked guilty, and Malachi wondered if he jacked up the price to receive a higher portion for himself. He had the money, even if it was an amount he'd not expected to be out.

Malachi drew his wallet from his inside vest pocket and pulled out the notes and coins without protest. Blevins called for his assistant to come forward from where he'd been quietly observing the maneuver with his head in an account book, made out a receipt and had his assistant sign it as the witness, then drew up quitclaim deeds for the three properties. He gave him the maps and directions to find the claims, warned him to watch what he ate up on the mountain, as poisonous plants abounded, and with everything duly witnessed, shook hands with the new owner and wished him luck. Malachi saw him gazing through the window as he climbed aboard his horse, and leading the mule, headed up the street and towards the center of the town.

He took a quick inventory in his head of how much cash he had left and how many supplies he still needed to live comfortably for the next month or so. He stopped at the first general store he saw and got what he considered necessary. The store owner gazed at the man's empty sleeve but made no comment, just collected the items called out, added up the bill, and told the stranger he would extend credit if necessary up to the amount of thirty dollars to any miner down on his luck. An amount above that number, he got a share of the mining claim. Malachi looked at him closely but nodded his head that he understood. He didn't plan to buy on credit unless he had to. He tied the stuffed burlap bag holding his purchases to the mule's pack, climbed into the saddle and rode out of town.

The sun was shining sporadically through the branches of the trees as he guided his horse and mule up the incline along the makeshift road beside the creek. Along the route he saw busy miners working their sluice boxes or lounging under a tree with a midday smoke. These were hard men; toughened and fired in the furnace of backbreaking work; some he suspected were deserters from the army, both Northern and Southern, maybe a few like himself with a legitimate discharge in his wallet. He saw a few women, and some children, but they were outnumbered, possibly twenty to one in this wilderness at the foot of the mighty stone mountains.

Malachi stopped twice and asked directions, receiving suspicious, curt answers, but satisfied that he was still on the right road. The path left the creek at several places and circled around large boulders, and he feared he might get lost. When he thought he was nearing Jethro Belton's former claim, he became more wary, thinking that Potter might be suspicious of a stranger appearing from nowhere with a horse and mule, but the man scarcely looked up from his work. Malachi hailed him and waved, observing closely the flimsy building and the leaning outhouse. It didn't look like much from the road, but Malachi knew that gold was here, for he had a piece of it in his secret pocket.

He knew from his education on the origin of precious metals that down river, only small dust or flecks would be found; the mother lode would be higher up somewhere, so he wasn't mourning the loss of Belton's claim. With any luck at all, he'd find enough dust to keep him through the winter months. He'd dig through his old schoolbook soon, read again about the geology of the unknown heights and look for signs of silver or copper. He had no doubt there were riches to be found in the mountains. His career thus far had centered on the final product of the metals involved: jewelry, time pieces, snuff boxes, coffee and tea pots; he had experience with them all, but couldn't work at his trade with only five fingers. He sighed. If only he hadn't read that summons to appear for the draft, but then he thought, with a frown of regret, that the soldiers would've picked him up, and he'd have been dragged into the Army, anyway.

He stopped in a shady glen to rest the horse and mule. He got down and drew his map from his pocket, looking for the landmarks that the agent had told him about. According to the paper, he was about a mile from his first claim. He sat beneath a tree and ate some crackers, a hunk of goat's cheese and sliced meat. He washed them down with apple cider he'd bought at the store in town. His thoughts returned to the letter he'd received from his brother, Elisha, in Springfield, Illinois, telling him that he would forward his share of the shop to his bank, when he got a permanent address.

The silversmith business of Clements and Sons had been founded by their grandfather in Albemarle County, Virginia, in the last century, but the sons had decided to move west and settled in Kaskaskia, Illinois, thence to Springfield when it became the capital of the state. Malachi and his brother had grown up in the shop and apprenticed at the age of seven. He knew no other business except for plowing and growing a few crops. He was a town-raised boy, but he supposed he could learn to live in the wilderness, with the future uncertain. He knew he couldn't go home, watch his brother at work and have his neighbors pity him and whisper behind his back.

He rose, mounted the horse and rode until he saw the large cottonwood tree with the slash marks and red paint marking the boundary of his claim. He turned left off the road and toward the sound of rushing water. He looked to the right of the creek banks to a small clearing and saw the one-room rude cabin that had been abandoned. He rode to the front door, dismounted and tied his horse and mule to a tree limb.

The logs were crudely cut and laid, but they looked substantial enough. The chimney was made of river stones, possibly gathered by the original owner. The sluice box, a long ramp-like affair out of flat timber, with battens to catch the heavy particles of gold, was weathered and probably needed repair, but it was now his. He walked around the perimeter looking for signs of human or animal tracks. He wasn't an experienced tracker, but he'd been taught the signs of bear, deer and wolves. He saw none.

The ground around the house was layered with dead leaves and pine cones from previous seasons, and a bare dirt track led to the sluice box, marking where the miner had come and gone in his daily work. He found an outhouse in the back yard and made use of it. It had spider webs, and the wood was rotting, but he would have time to fix that problem. The entire area was surrounded by bristlecone pines and spruce and chokecherry bushes. The creek flowed swiftly with two sandy islands in the center and large rounded rocks scattered around like a giant hand had thrown them into the water.

Malachi stepped cautiously upon the two wooden planks that served as a porch and opened the door to his cabin. It wasn't locked from the outside. He stood a moment letting his eyes become accustomed to the dim interior. He could see directly in front of him the fireplace with some kindling and what looked to be old rags or newspapers in a box nearby. Hanging from the mantle were some utensils, pots and a rusty iron skillet. He saw a table of about two feet by four feet rectangular shape, with a bench on either side. There were no chairs.

A few shelves and pegs hung on the walls, clearly functional but not luxurious, by any stretch of the imagination. A single bunk bed sat against the wall near the fireplace with a dirty straw mattress, bearing marks of sweat or blood. He passed it by. A thick coat of dust covered the whole, and spider webs were visible through the ray of afternoon sun shining in the open window. He looked up into the chimney to see if there were bird's nests or dirt clogs hidden among the stones, but he could see the blue of the sky through the dark chamber. He decided to climb on the roof and try to clean it, anyway. He sure didn't want to burn the only home he had on his first night on his claim.

He checked on the horse and mule and found them contentedly munching on the grass. He removed the saddle and leaned it against the house, then relieved the mule of his burden, stacking the goods just inside the open door of the cabin. He opened the packs and found an old cloth. He cut a limb from a tree and tied the cloth to the limb. He then found a tree near enough in the back yard that he could climb onto the roof and walked to the chimney. He stuffed the cloth inside using the limb stretched to its limit and decided that would have to be sufficient. It was an awkward business, and twice he thought he would lose his balance and tumble from the roof. The thought occurred to him that he was totally alone, and no one would care if he lay for hours on his back, paralyzed and in the sun. He shuddered at the thought. He felt a tingle in his stump and scratched it. The bandage was now gray and dirty, but no sign of blood came through.

He threw the limb and cloth to the ground and climbed down by way of the tree. He went inside and examined the kindling and old papers in the wooden box, arranged a few in the fireplace and lit it with a sulfur match. It caught fire nicely. Soon a warm blaze filled the room, and he was satisfied. He pulled the mattress from the bed, took it outside and set it afire. While he watched it burn, he gave the horse and mule a rubdown with the cloth from the limb. He took them to the creek for a long drink before hobbling them under the trees where there was plenty of verdant grass to nibble on. He stomped out the remaining ashes of the mattress fire and covered them with soil.

He searched in the pack for a bucket, took it to the stream and filled it with water. In the house, he washed the table, benches and the front surface of the fireplace with water and lye soap. He hunched on his knees and scrubbed the floor until the sun threw long shadows across the room. He looked around and decided he had done enough for one day. His stubble of an arm ached from unaccustomed use.

Using some bacon and corn meal from his pack, he made a simple supper of bacon and corn fritters, with hot fragrant coffee. He was so tired he didn't mind sleeping on the hard floor, wrapped in a blanket. The warmth and scent of the fire soon filled his senses, and he slept through the night.

— 3 —

The sun was already above the horizon when Malachi awoke and stretched his limbs. He rolled out of the blanket, shivering in the frosty morning air. He poked at the fire to find it had burned itself out during the night, and he used the remaining kindling and newspapers to relight it. Digging out flour, salt and lard, he proceeded to make some biscuits, using his own utensils and flimsy tin oven instead of those at the fireplace. When the coffee was finished, he poured himself a cup. He took a cloth and removed the kitchen utensils from the mantle, wishing he'd done that before building the fire, and set his oven at the side of the flames. He placed the tin of biscuits in to bake, while he went to the stream for water. Pouring a small amount into a basin, he washed the previous owner's kitchen things and set them on a cloth on the table to dry.

He went out to the horse and mule to see that

they were alright. They were happily eating grass, so he came back and finished his breakfast, sitting in the doorway afterwards with a cup of coffee in his hand and looking out at the tranquil scene in front of the cabin. He wondered if there were trout in the brook. His thoughts returned to Jethro Belton and his dreams of gold. It wasn't the same claim, but he could imagine the man working the sluice and finding the small nugget of gold. He imagined his glee and excitement. Would he find gold in these mountains, Malachi wondered, or only trouble and death? He shrugged away his melancholy thoughts and rose. He quickly washed his cup and coffee pot, threw the dirty water out the door and packed his things away on the mule.

With the horse saddled and mounted, and the mule following behind, Malachi set out to find his second property. On the trail, he passed a claim with men working; a woman and two children were standing near a tent. Malachi imagined it must be rough to live in a tent; he wondered why the man hadn't built a cabin for his family, but supposed it was none of his affair. He came to the markings that pointed to his claim and looked with disappointment at the burned ruin of the cabin. Several trees near the cabin had also been burned, leaving scarred trunks and fallen pine cones on the ground. He'd been warned by the agent, but still it was a depressing sight.

He dismounted from the horse and tied the animals to a tree. He unsaddled the brute and took the pack from the mule. There were some unburned logs and lumber left among the ashes, and he wondered if rain or humans had put out the fire before it had completely consumed the house. He pulled them from the wreckage and set them aside. The ashes and dust fell around him like an early morning fog. The sluice had been destroyed, but there were some usable raw planks nearby. He added them to his pile of lumber, wiping his forehead as he realized the sun was quite warm; and finished, he sat down in the dirt to rest for a time.

He noticed a high bluff or wall several yards from the creek, forming a natural barrier against a stand of trees. It appeared to be an ancient bend in the stream, where at one time long ago the water had flooded and left a soft cliff of sandy loam. He walked to the creek and estimated if there was the possibility of the same thing happening twice. He moved around the area, climbed to the top of the cliff and gazed at the winding stream as it flowed downhill. He stomped on the high ground and found it solid.

He laughed to himself, slapping his leg in exultation. Dust flew from his pants, but it didn't matter. He felt he'd made a decision that could change his life from this moment forward.

He removed his shovel and pick axe from the pack. He pinned his empty sleeve more securely to the underarm of his shirt and lifted the axe. His arm had grown very strong from constant use, and the axe was hardly heavy in his hand. He swung it at the sandy soil, using one arm and half the other, the metal instrument biting the dirt shallowly at first, but he soon got into a rhythm that felt comfortable. Cutting off tree roots, and removing the occasional stone, he worked for half an hour before he took his first rest. At one point, he was forced to crack a large, brittle ledge of stone to continue his endeavors. He hefted one fragment he removed, wondering at the glittering shards in the heavy mass, before tossing it towards the water. "Fool's gold," he muttered. Across the creek, he caught a glint in the trees. Narrowing his eyes, and peering carefully, he looked to see if anyone was there.

"Hallo," he cried. "Neighbor? You there?"

There was no answer. He looked around to get his bearings and began again. He'd dug about two feet into the loamy soil when he decided it was time for a longer break. Digging in his pouch, he found a couple of leftover biscuits and opened a can of peaches. Water from the clear mountain stream satisfied his thirst.

By working and resting, then working again, he had about seven feet of earth dug out with the soil piled high to one side of the entrance. He could use it later to level a low place he'd seen in the paddock, although he'd have to construct a cart of some sort to transport it. A second time, he thought someone might be across the creek. As the sun waned, he was certain someone coughed in the cooling, mountain air. He paused, watching for any movement, but all was still, and there were no more sounds, other than those the forest normally makes. Besides, the stream burbled quite loudly, and many sounds were probably hidden by the rushing waters.

He thought again how to use the excess soil, as there was quite a lot, perhaps as a barrier to hold back the water in case of a flood, but he wasn't decided on how it would be accomplished, yet. He fed his horse some oats and built a fire nearby, then he cooked a hasty meal, watered the animals and crawled in his blankets, his muscles aching, and was soon dead to the world.

****

Up early the next morning, Malachi took several of the planks from the ruined sluice and shored up the roof and walls of his dugout. He dug another five feet, going farther down into the dirt, digging up tree roots and hitting some gravel and rocks. Occasionally, he sifted through the dirt for signs of gold dust, silver or copper, but found none. He widened the cave and shored the walls again, his room becoming larger and deeper into the earth. When it was about twenty feet wide and eight feet deep, he tested the roof and walls and found them sufficient. He rested for over an hour, sitting under the shade of the trees. A red squirrel chattered overhead, and at the sound of a broken twig, a deer appeared, a doe from its build. A bird twittered, and the deer belted through the woods, disappearing into the shadowy depths.

Using the rest of his lumber and planks, Malachi nailed them together making a sort of wooden cabin inside the sod walls. He fashioned a two-foot wide overhang to keep out the rain or snow, then stopped for the night. He lay a fire at the entrance to the sod house and prepared some food, a hoecake from some ground meal and a portion of beans. He was too tired to do more, and he fell to his bed and lay as though dead, his back, shoulders and arms aching with pain and exhaustion. He'd never endeavored to do such hard labor before, and his recent wounds made him feel weak and tired. He decided to rest on the morrow and maybe try the creek for fish.

He rose late in the day, the sun already high in the sky. His body ached with the previous day's exertion. His wounded arm felt like a lead weight; but surprisingly he was invigorated by the hard labor. He looked at the raw blisters on his hand and groaned. He should've remembered to buy a pair of heavy leather gloves. He remembered the years of toil over a table working with his father's tools and fashioning delicate jewelry for the ladies, or carving intricate flowers or leaves in a silver tray. He swallowed the bitter gall in his throat, telling himself those days were gone forever, and it would only hurt more to remember them. As a distraction, he went to the creek and bathed himself in the icy water and put on clean clothes. Afterwards, he carefully wrapped his hand in a clean cloth, using his teeth to draw it tight, and covered it with a sock.

A breakfast of bacon, fried potatoes and onions, together with hot coffee, renewed his fortitude, and Malachi twisted a small wire into a hook and cut it off with his thin knife from the scabbard in his boot. Using a length of twine, his teeth and his one hand, he tied the wire hook to make a fishing jig. He found a strong sapling, cut it down and stripped the branches to make himself a fishing pole. Once at the creek, he threw the line as far as he could into the water, then sat on the bank and waited. He thought something moved on the other side of the stream but told himself it was only a wild creature of the forest.

The line floated for about twenty minutes when he got a nibble. He yanked the pole high above the water with his one hand but lost the fish when it flipped from his hook and plunged into the depths with a splash. Rather than feeling discouraged, Malachi was exhilarated. At least there were fish in the water. He reset the hook with a tied twist of straw and a feather he found on the ground. He threw his line back into the water.

By noon he had four nice-sized trout on his fire. He determined he'd eat as much fish as he could stand and save his precious supplies. What was free for the taking was meant to be taken. He laughed out loud and was surprised by the sound of his own voice. He started singing a song he'd learned in the Army to keep him company.

He pulled his steel mining pan from his pack and knelt at the water's edge to try his luck in the soft sand and loose gravel. Crouched over his pan, he was careless of his surroundings and jumped, startled, when he heard a man's voice. The pan fell into the water with a splash.

"Hallo, the camp."

Malachi looked up and saw a man approaching from the north. He was dressed in a dark blue wool shirt, with suspenders and brown trousers. His hair was blond, the color darker close to his head, and tangled, as if rarely combed. A spotty beard covered the lower half of his face, the color matching that on top of his head. His footwear sported copious layers of soil. Malachi was instantly alert and cursed himself for leaving his weapon in the dugout. He felt the small pistol in his vest pocket and knew he had the knife in his boot, so was reassured. He eased his back and rose to his full height.

"Hallo, yourself, stranger." He gazed around to see if others were hovering nearby but saw or heard nothing.

"Don't be alarmed." The stranger remained still, not moving toward Malachi's camp. He scratched at his side, making a smacking noise with his lips, as if putting his words together, then pointed into the trees. "Got my own claim up river there a ways toward Astra. Got lonely so decided I'd go to Denver for a few days, collect some supplies. Saw your dugout. Now, that's a clever way to live, cozy in winter, pleasant in summer."

It was more a question than a statement, but Malachi didn't answer. The man nervously shifted his feet.

"Nabors is my name. Renzo Nabors. Been here almost since the beginning. Not at the same place, though. Drifted up from Cherry Creek once the pilgrims started building it into a town." He shrugged and looked over his shoulder at the forest behind him. " 'Fraid most of the gold's gone. Been thinking of moving on toward the west."

He raised one eyebrow, and Malachi felt he should say something. "I haven't been here long; just a few days. Name's Malachi Clements. Pleased to meet you."

"Say, don't want to disturb you, Mister Clements, but I could use a cup of coffee if you've a mind. Gets cold in the mountains, traveling. But, just say the word, and I'll be on my way."

Malachi thought of his own solitude and the man seemed friendly enough. He relaxed.

"Come on up to the camp, Nabors. I could use a break. It's not much to look at, but it's comfortable enough. I'll get a fire going." He walked up the slope to his fire and placed a couple of small pieces of kindling on his dying coals. He scrounged in his pack and found the coffee pot and his grinder. Setting the grinder and bag of coffee beans on the ground, he shook the empty pot, giving the stranger a quick glance.

"Hand that to me Clements, I'll fill it with

water."

Malachi offered him the pot and saw up close that the man had a ragged scar on his face, cutting close to his brown eyes. Keeping his attention on Nabors' actions, he poked the fire to get it going more smoothly and ducked into the pack to reassure himself that his weapon was handy.

Nabors brought the pot from the creek and set it on the ground near the fire, talking as he stirred the coals with a stick.

"Came from Kentucky. Read about the gold strike in the newspaper and sold my business. I'm a clock maker by trade. Not much call for clocks once the war started at Sumter. Didn't make much of a soldier; got wounded at Bull Run." He rubbed his face. "I came out west. You a soldier, too?" He gazed curiously at Malachi's sleeve.

"Used to be." Malachi didn't elaborate as he turned the coffee grinder. Once he had enough, he returned the grinder to his bag. He put some grounds in the pot and placed it on the fire. The silence was broken only by the birds and the stamp of the mule's hoof in the shelter.

"I see you've got a mule. Donkeys are better for hauling a pack. Mules are too temperamental of a morning. My pa got kicked by a mule and had a limp from then on." Nabors sat in the dirt and gazed across the river as though thinking of the past.

Malachi drew the coffee pot from the stove with a cloth and poured two cups. He heard the stamp of his mule's hoof, and it drew his attention.

"Name's Caesar. The mule, that is. The horse doesn't have a name. He's most as stubborn as the mule."

"Known a few women that way." Nabors held up his cup as if in a toast, and he chuckled. His beard caught the light where coffee trailed down the front. He lifted his arm to press it to his chin, soaking up the moisture. "You feeding your animals any of the native plants?"

"Why?" Malachi had thought of collecting edibles from around his camps. He knew there were sometimes plants that could flavor stews, but he'd not had a chance to survey the flora to any degree. He let his animals eat what they would.

"Watch for the lupine seeds. Larkspurs, too. They make mighty pretty flowers, but let your animals get into 'em, and you might lose 'em."

"Larkspurs? Flowers, aren't they? You're saying they're poisonous?"

"When blooming, mostly, or when wet. You planning on any sheep?"

"Sheep, man? Of course not."

Nabors laughed. "Most don't, but we've got some sneezeweed about, and it won't hurt your horse, but a man might lose a sheep or two in a stand of sneezeweed."

"How do I recognize it?" Malachi let his eyes roam the area, searching, even though he wouldn't know it if he found it.

"Yea high." Nabors held his hand about three

feet above the ground. "Orange flowers, darker centers, with hairy seeds. You see it, you'll know." He tossed back the rest of his coffee, stood, stretched, and placed his cup on the ground.

"Guess I'll be getting on down the creek. It'll be dark soon. Thanks for the coffee, Clements."

Malachi watched the man saunter off into the woods, his hand once again scratching where he had before, until he disappeared into the trees.

****

Malachi remained at his dugout home for four more days and nights, making improvements and hiding a small cache of tinned food for later use. Early on the fifth day, he rose before dawn, saddled the horse, and put the pack on the mule. He left a board nailed to the entrance to his cabin noting that it was the property of Malachi Clements. He knew that wouldn't keep the intruders away, but hoped that they would soon realize from the signs of usage that the site was occupied.

Up and up, the trail wound through the trees and boulders, the creek now several yards to the left off the beaten road. The trail was narrow and, in some places, hardly wide enough for the horse and mule, so Malachi got off and led them along the path. It widened into a vast, open space, and he took a deep breath, amazed at the scene laid out before him. Below him and to the horizon, he could see forests and mountain ridges. To the west, white, puffy clouds sailed across the dark blue sky. It was an amazing sight, one that he would remember for the rest of his days. It was his first true sighting of the great Rocky Mountain range, and below him was the silvery winding stream called Fossil Creek, carving its own path to the sea. He couldn't see any working miners or their cabins, hidden by the thick forests as they were, but he knew they were there. One dominant mountain among all the rest was covered with snow, and Malachi gazed his fill at the wondrous sight before moving on up the trail.

He turned one sharp bend to be confronted by a blockage made of fallen rocks and tree limbs, no doubt caused by a small avalanche during the past winter. He laboriously circled around it, several times having to take his axe from his pack mule and chop a trail through the heavy brush, but he finally came back to the road. On the left he saw the now-familiar boundary markers and knew that he was on his own land once more. He felt over-whelmed with gratitude to be so close to the open space that showed the amazing vistas of the high mountains. He pulled on the horse's reins and turned to where he knew the stream must be.

With delicate and slow motions, he guided the animals through a narrow opening in the giant boulders and tall pine trees to a clearing that was obviously a miner's claim, surrounded by deep forest, and on the opposite bank, a hundred feet or more, a tall cliff. Scrub pine, aspen trees and scattered chokecherry bushes projected from cracks in the sandstone and granite surfaces. The whole cliff glowed with a dark russet, red-brown color from the sun's rays. Malachi could see seams of dark brown and lighter colored minerals, all deposited by some ancient river that had flowed through the area and left behind striations and grooves to tell of the ancient glaciers that once covered the ground.

The clearing was small but had a faded green, painted, one-room cabin with a stone chimney, an outhouse, and a shed and corrals for the animals. It was obvious the previous owner had cared for the place well. He could see a trail leading to the right, which must be the path to the village of Astra. He would check that out later. There was the mandatory sluice box and what looked to be a dock for a boat or canoe. He hadn't thought the stream deep enough for rowing. Malachi stepped from the saddle, and he knew why the agent in Denver City had said it was his favorite. It was perfect; every man's dream of home, high in the invigorating, clear air of the mountains. According to the agent, he owned five acres of land, mostly thick forest. For now, he needed to see about his animals, for they were breathing harder in the thin, moist air.

He realized he was having a bit of struggle with his own breath. He'd learned a valuable lesson; don't ride up the slopes too quickly. He tied the horse to a sapling and took the mule to the water to drink, and then led him to the front of the cabin and unloaded the pack from his back. He walked to the corrals to see if they were secure, and noting they were, he led the mule to it and released him. He went back for the horse and repeated the process, laying the saddle and blanket near the door of the cabin. When the animals appeared calm and their breathing normal, Malachi turned his attention to the cabin.

It was a near replica of the one on his first claim, the one the previous owner had named Brinkley's Manor. As he stood in the doorway, he could see the woman's touch in the room. There were dusty gingham curtains on the window and a faded, matching cloth on the table. It was half covered with pots and pans of different sizes. A small table and two chairs stood in front of the east window where they would get the early morning sunshine. Malachi could imagine a man and woman sitting there eating their breakfast, and he was intrigued. A quick remembrance of Rose-anne's sweet smile crossed his mind, and he brushed it aside. There were two crude, wide beds, one he assumed for the married couple, and one for the children, with a heavy cord drawn between them for privacy. A blanket lay on the floor in a layer of gray dust. He was very pleased with his find; even if he didn't discover gold, he could live here content and happy in his mountain shelter, enjoying the bracing climate and the beautiful surroundings.

He left the cabin and walked the perimeter. A shed attached to the corrals provided stalls for two animals, and it contained several bales of old hay and oats in burlap sacks. There was a farm wagon parked at one end. He walked around the back and saw a canoe under a lean-to addition. He'd never seen a canoe up close so examined it closely. It seemed to be made of birch and animals hides. This roused his curiosity, so he went to the edge of the creek. It looked deep, narrow and swift.

About thirty yards upstream, the deepest water hugged the far bank, and a large sand bar projected from the near one. Animal and human prints were visible in the sand. He searched for evidence of placer deposits along the shore. A rise of tree-covered earth, buried in the shadows, with the side partially cut away, revealed a buff color, indicating loess, which might indicate mineral deposits. A sluice box similar to the first was built along the sand underneath a large cottonwood tree. Malachi walked along its side and saw a large abandoned beaver dam. He couldn't fathom whether the man had built the sluice near the beaver dam, or the beavers had used the abandoned sluice to build against.

He saw something shiny in the underwater sand and stooped to pick it up. It was a silver coin, minted by the United States government and dated five years previously. Malachi let out a yelp of joy that echoed back from the opposite high cliff of solid rock. Clearly, the coin had been dropped by a human; possibly the previous owner, while he was working in the sluice box. He rubbed the sand off and put it in his pocket. It was enough to buy a few weeks more of groceries without having to use his dwindling funds.

Intrigued, he ran to the cabin, removed from his pack a pair of knee-high India rubber boots that he'd bought for the purpose and changed into them. He put another flannel shirt over the one he wore for warmth and went back to the creek. Wading into the icy water, he took a stick and stirred the sand. About eight inches farther north, he found another silver coin, then another. Half buried in the sand, and in the branches, twigs and leaves of the beaver dam, there were the remains of a deerskin pouch, its drawstring intact, but a small hole possibly pierced by the gnawing of a beaver's teeth.

Malachi drew it from the dirt and opened it. There were numerous pieces of silver of different denominations. He sorted through the various dimes, quarters, and half-dollars to discover a cache of one-dollar coins; over thirty dollars in minted silver. He frantically dug for several more minutes, but there were no more. Jeffrey Townsend, the previous owner, must have hidden his poke in the beaver dam, or deep in the sand near his sluice box. Why did Townsend leave it behind when he left for the city? The agent in Denver City, Clarence Blevins, had told him that Townsend left in a hurry because his wife was ill. He must have expected to come back, or he would never have left his money behind.

Pushing the pouch under the waist band of his pants, Malachi saw a minute grain of gleaming sand. He scooped a handful of the sand into his hand and let it slip through his fingers. Gold dust! One tiny grain, but where one was, many more were sure to be. His heart thumping, he knelt, sifted the sand for several inches around the spot and found a few more gold flecks. As though turned into a wild man, he began to tear away at the beaver dam, throwing sticks and twigs and leaves into the air in his effort to find more shiny sand particles but found none. He moved to the edge of the creek, sat on dry sand and watched the debris drift downstream. He was sweating, and his breath was coming in shallow gulps. He'd forgotten the high altitude. He must calm down and be patient, he told himself. He had plenty of time, now that he had money to spend in the town.

As if coming out of a dream, Malachi noticed that the shadows had deepened, and the sun was no longer shining on the high cliff across the stream. It was growing dark, and he hadn't prepared for the night. He wearily rose from his sitting position and trudged up the incline so as not to start his heart palpitating again, for it was a scary feeling, not being able to draw a deep breath into his lungs. He felt in his pocket, and the pouch and money were still there. He was wet, cold, and his feet felt numb; he must make a fire and get warm. His stomach rumbled with hunger, and he remembered he hadn't eaten since starting from the second camp early in the morning

Slowly, pacing himself, he entered the cabin and threw the sticks and kindling he'd found in his path onto the floor in front of the fireplace. He took his sulfur matches from his pack and laid a fire in the fireplace. He didn't attempt to climb on the roof to see if the chimney was clear, for he was too tired and weak from his earlier struggles with the beaver dam. He lit the kindling, and it blazed up with a yellow and red flame. The smoke flew naturally up the chimney, and Malachi said a prayer of gratitude. He peeled his wet clothes and boots from his body, and using a soft, clean towel, dried himself. He wrapped up in a couple of blankets and was soon asleep on the floor.

Dreams of war visited Malachi that night. The battle surged all around him, with the swish of a bullet near his right ear, and almost at the same time, an explosion of pain in his left arm. He looked down and saw that his hand was gone. Ducking under the scant shelter of a fallen log, he took his belt from his pants and wrapped a tourniquet around his upper arm. A mist appeared before him, blurring his sight, and the blackness overwhelmed him.

The former soldier sat up and looked around him, the nightmare fading into the shadows of his mind, as he realized that he was high in the mountains of Colorado Territory, and the heat was coming from the two blankets and the slowly burning wood of the fireplace. He threw the covers aside and went to the bucket of cool water that he'd earlier drawn from the creek. He took a long, invigorating swallow and knew the pain in his belly was from hunger. He scooped the rest of his branches into the fire. He would have to cut some wood tomorrow, as the small pickings from the ground wouldn't last long.

He searched in his pack for some beef jerky and chewed it slowly while forcing himself to remember the dream. He'd discovered if he brought the memories back and examined them closely, some of the anguish and fear retreated. The dreams had, over time, become less acute and appeared less often. He ate a second piece of jerky and took another long drink of water, and his hunger was appeased for a while. The smell of dust and the rancid odor of decayed straw in the mattresses was in the air.

He rose and found some clean clothes and dressed. He lifted his weapon and propped the barrel against his left shoulder, holding the stock securely with the elbow stub. He went out to check on the animals. There seemed a million stars in the sky overhead. He couldn't see the moon but supposed it was hidden by the high cliff because of the brightness of the area.

The horse was lying down and the mule standing with his back to the shed. Malachi soothed them and looked around for danger, but everything appeared well outside the cabin. He went back in and lay on his rumpled blankets, pondering the silver coins. He pictured the man and his wife working the sluice, while the boys ran, shouting, in and out of the trees. Gray smoke drifted from the chimney, and chickens plucked particles of corn from the ground.

His imagination began to work as he conjured up scenes of bandits or train robbers who might have dropped the pouch in their haste to escape capture by a sheriff's posse. Maybe, the pouch had drifted with the current from the high slopes and was caught in the beaver dam. He lay for a long time watching the flames as they died out, and afterwards, the glow from the coals turned a bright red then a dull gray color as the heat left them. He had no more wood to feed the fire, and soon he grew sleepy. He removed his boots but not his clothes. He rested on one blanket and spread the other over his body. In the distance, he could hear the hoot of an owl and the soothing, meandering stream outside his cabin walls.

He finally slept a good, clean sleep.

— 4 —

In contrast to the night before, Malachi woke with a chill. The coals in the fireplace were gray ashes. He knew he must get some wood for the fire. He pulled on his boots and dug his heavy wool coat from his pack, shivering in the cold air. He found his shovel, lifted the ashes onto it and carried them outside. He first checked on the animals, but they seemed contented munching on the grass of the corral.

He unearthed the axe and walked to the edge of the forest, holding the axe in his left elbow stub and braced against his shoulder. He picked up two rather large limbs, and careful not to get scratched from the twigs and sharp edges, dragged them closer to the cabin. Carefully balancing himself, he swung the axe in an arc and split the lesser branches from the trunks, then chopped the limbs into small, manageable lengths.

He lay his axe down and toted the kindling into

the house a small load at a time. He went back for more heavy limbs, and cut them up in the same manner. He realized that his breath was shallow; his heart was racing; and sweat was seeping through his clothes, causing him to shiver in the early morning fog. After an hour, he had enough wood for a couple of days, if he was conservative with it.

He built a fire in the fireplace and made a pot of coffee. He felt overly warm, took off his coat and lay it on his blankets. He cut a few strips of bacon, and the smell made him nauseous. Recognizing that he'd caught a fever, he hurriedly ate and drank then crawled into the blankets. He watched the flames for a few minutes but was soon asleep. He woke twice during the day, once when he was shaking with cold and his feet numb. He stumbled to the wood and built up the fire, then lay back down. Next, he woke feeling hot, and his throat was dry. He drank some tepid water from the bucket and, mumbling to himself, crawled back into the blankets.

The nightmare came back, more vivid than before, and he awoke in pain and fever. His stomach was cramping, and he doubled up to ease the discomfort, thinking he might have eaten something poisonous. He screamed out loud, and the sound startled him. He jerked up and reached for his rifle but couldn't find it. The slowly dying fire sent ghostly shadows on the walls and furnishings, and he cowered in the room, shaking in fear.

Again, he saw in his mind the hospital room and heard the sounds of moaning, as the men lay dying from their wounds. He felt of his stub with his one hand and rubbed it gently. That gave him the courage he needed, and he crawled to the wood and pitched some more onto the coals. The flames burst upward with a shower of sparks, alive and casting out the demons that haunted him. He made his way to the blankets and rolled up in them.

When next he awoke, Malachi was clear headed, and the chills and fever were gone. The sun was high overhead, and the forest was quiet except for the soft rustle of leaves in the slight breeze blowing from the south. He wondered how many days had passed while he was ill. One? Two? He would never know. He was hungry, and he sliced some bacon and found a potato that proved to be dark and rotten in the center. He threw it outside toward the outhouse. He sliced another one and some onions, and fried them in lard until they were brown and soft. He opened a tin of beans and ate them from the can.

Refreshed by the food, he went outside and gave his horse a small container of oats. The mule seemed to be content in the corral digging among the roots and grass. He walked to the remnants of the beaver dam and noticed that the level of the water seemed to have receded in the days when he was sleeping. He left the creek and decided to examine the cabin while he regained his strength. He first pulled the old mattresses from the cots and set them afire outside. The smell was pungent, and the gray smoke curled toward the sky. While he watched the flames, he examined the outside of the cabin for cracks or mold. The man had built well. It was in better shape than the first one he'd cleaned.

When the mattresses were ashes, he covered them with dirt and went back into the house. He didn't feel up to scrubbing the contents, so pulled out his cord and hooks, found a small sapling and went fishing. The water was deep near the sluice box, and he threw his line into the water. He caught two large trout and one smaller one. He cooked one of the large ones for his dinner, left the other two in the frigid waters of the stream and took a nap in the afternoon. The silence of the forest was soothing, and he awoke refreshed and strong again. He chopped some more wood for the fire and cooked the last of the fish for his evening meal. He made some corn fritters to accompany the fish and drank two cups of coffee. He slept peacefully that night.

Malachi Clements was up before the dawn and stirring about in the cabin. He built up the fire and went to the creek for a pail of fresh water. When he smelled his underarms, he decided to take a cold dip in the water and wash his hair and beard. He donned clean underwear, a shirt and socks, his last pair of clean trousers, and dug out the large metal tub that was in the cabin. He strung a cord between two trees where the full sun would hit the clothes and washed his belongings. When they were hanging on the line, he dumped the water near the door, making a temporary puddle on the grass.

Somewhat refreshed from his bath, he walked up the path, gathering limbs and branches. He stuffed his pockets full of pine cones. He learned that it was easier to gather downed wood than to use his meager strength to cut it with an axe, another lesson learned about wilderness living. He rested from his labors while sitting on the front step of the cabin. He thought of his brother and the silversmith shop they had founded together. He began to hum. Then, laughing at his own inexperience and ignorance of the mountains, he began to talk; it didn't matter what he said; there was no one about to hear him. He started talking to Jethro Belton, the man who'd given him the gold nugget. He told him of the silence of the mountains, of the stream and the beaver dam, and finally, with a smile of gratitude, he told him of his find of silver coins. He gazed into the sky when he saw a large bird fly by; and as though speaking a prayer, he raised his lone hand, spread his fingers wide, and he said, "Thank you, Jethro, wherever you are; thank you."

He rose, and taking a piece of the previous owner's burlap, he fashioned a large bag to hang over his shoulder so he could carry more wood chips and pine cones. He gathered small branches and filled the bag full before returning to the cabin and resting again.

He filled a basin with water and heated it on the fire. When it was warm enough to suit him, he washed the Townsend woman's kitchen utensils and flatware. He scrubbed the tables and chairs from top to bottom, and finding himself once more exhausted, pulled one of the chairs to the door. Pouring himself a cup of coffee, he gratefully took time to rest. He assumed he'd get used to the thin air and not tire so easily.

With the afternoon grown lazy, and the dregs of his coffee cold, he lay down and rested his eyes. Sometime later, refreshed, he guiltily got to his feet and resumed scrubbing the contents of the cabin. The floor he left for another day. Late that night, he took the silver coins from the beaver-nibbled pouch and counted them again. He noticed that the dates on the minted coins covered several years, so they wouldn't be traced to the same source. He put them in a small leather bag that he'd hoped would hold his gold dust. He threw the old bag onto the fire and watched it burn. Gone up in smoke was any evidence that he'd not brought them with him from the east.

He felt a sigh of relief well up inside, and he finally felt he could begin to make plans.

He knew that he'd been gone from the first cabin at least a week and needed to get back. To keep his claims, it was important to be seen by his neighbors working the sluice boxes. He saw the clean utensils and got an idea. He didn't need duplicate sets. There was no reason he couldn't trade them for other things he needed. He'd brought his own necessary cooking equipment in his pack. With bartering and spending the coins wisely, he could make his funds last for a year or more. He got up and found a rather large burlap bag from his pack and put two pots, a pewter plate, a skillet and some flatware in the bag. He hid the coins deep in a bag of corn meal.

The next morning, Malachi saddled his horse and hefted the pack onto his mule, leaving the large bag with the Townsend equipment dangling on the side, securely tied to the pack, where it rattled and bounced with the mule's movements. He closed and locked the door and started up the trail to the village of Astra. It wasn't far, about ten miles, and he stopped twice on the way to gaze at the magnificent vistas of the high Rocky Mountain Range. He again saw the beauty of the single, snow-covered mountain peak in the distance and wondered if it had a name.

He rode into the village of Astra about mid-afternoon, his breathing shallow and the horse and mule tired and struggling for deep breaths. He looked about him at the squalor of the place. There was a large wooden building with a sign that said Akins General Store, and a stable and several saloons. The buildings were a combination of rude tar paper shacks, tents and small log cabins. The houses of the permanent inhabitants seemed to be strung like beads up and down a central avenue, and the town scattered at the base of a hill, with an intersection separating the haves from the have-nots. He rode steadily forward, headed to the general store, but was slowed by women standing at the entrance to what was clearly a brothel calling to him. If anyone noticed his empty sleeve, he wasn't aware of it.

He stopped in front of the store and tied his horse and mule to the hitching post. He took the burlap bag off the pack animal and went into the establishment. There were four men and one woman in the room. The woman was clearly of the upper class, dressed in the fashion of the era, with a high neck bodice and a large, dark red silk skirt with a hoop and many petticoats underneath. One man wore a black frock coat and was probably her husband or brother. They seemed oddly out of place in the wilderness. The other two were clad in the same manner as Malachi, the overalls and denim pants of the miner. They had on plaid flannel shirts and brown boots, scuffed and worn. Malachi walked to the front of the store with his bag hoisted over his right shoulder.

One man stood behind the counter and was obviously the proprietor. He was dressed in a white shirt with a black string tie, had red garters around each sleeve and leather cuffs to protect the shirt's wrist cuffs from dirt and fraying. His trousers were brown corduroy. Malachi couldn't see his feet, but imagined that he wore the same type of shoes that he sold in his store. He glanced at the former soldier's sleeve but didn't grimace or blink in surprise. The woman stared at it, but Malachi was used to the gesture of pity shown in her eyes, and he ignored her.

"Good day, sirs, lady. I'm Malachi Clements, former soldier and silversmith. I've recently bought three mining claims in these mountains and need some supplies." He waited for a reaction, trusting they would deal with him politely.

"Three claims? Did you say three? What would a man do with three claims?" The man with the frock coat moved aggressively forward, which was puzzling, as anyone could have as many claims as they wanted, Malachi assumed.

"Why, the same thing that a man with one claim wants, Hezekiah. Gold. My name's Stockwell, Mr. Clements, Jason Stockwell. Welcome to Astra." This came from one of the men wearing suspenders over a green plaid shirt. He stepped out as though to stop the other man from advancing. He raised his right hand to shake, but noticed that Malachi had only one hand and it was holding the bag of utensils. He coughed and started to withdraw, but Malachi dropped his bag on the floor and shook hands.

"You're right, sir, I'm seeking gold, but first I need food." He laughed, hoping they'd join in to ease the tension in the room. The miners and the proprietor did, but the frock-coated gentleman frowned. The lady withdrew to the sewing notions counter, but continued to listen to the conversation. She pretended to look at the rolls of gingham and damask cloth, once picking up a card of buttons and laying it back down.

"What do you have in your bag, Mr. Clements?" the blue-shirted man asked, and looked closely at the bag. Malachi detected a degree of avarice in his eyes.

"Kitchen utensils and flatware. They were in the Townsend cabin, and I've a bountiful supply of my own. I thought I might barter with someone for the price of some lard, bacon and flour. Some sugar would be nice, too, either brown or cane." He looked at the proprietor as he spoke, but the man grimaced with displeasure. He apparently wasn't interested in used merchandise.

"Let's see what you have, Mr. Clements. I know a few miners who could perhaps use a skillet or pan." Jason Stockwell again took control of the conversation.

Malachi looked keenly at the proprietor, who walked from behind the counter and toward the lady, who was now looking at a jar of mixed sizes and colors of buttons. Malachi opened the bag, using his one hand and teeth to loosen the drawstring. He pulled out the pewter plate from the bag and set it on the counter, and reached for the next item, which was a large, slightly rusted iron skillet. One by one he took the contents from the bag. The final articles were a set of tarnished tableware, two pewter spoons, two wooden-handled table knives, and one large, silver serving spoon of inferior quality. He could have made one much better and with a fancier design if he had the necessary equipment in his shop.

"Not very good quality silver, I'm afraid; probably silver plate, made from an alloy, perhaps copper." Malachi didn't realize the lady was listening closely to his description. He'd assumed she was disinterested and ignoring the entire proceedings. She came back toward the counter, picked up the large spoon and looked at the intricate design on the handle. The frock-coated man watched her closely. The proprietor returned behind his counter.

"Did you say you were a silversmith, sir?" She fondled the spoon between thumb and forefinger. "Where are you from?" She gazed at Malachi with her big gray eyes.

"Springfield, Illinois, the capital city. You might remember that the president of the United States is from Springfield. My brother and I have a shop there, but you can see that I'm no longer able to follow my trade, so I decided to travel west for my fortune." He watched Frock Coat and was pleased with his reaction to the mention of the president and the silversmith shop in his hometown.

"Did you say that this isn't real silver? What did you say; it was made from an alloy? What's that, sir?" The lady put down the large spoon and took up a knife. She ran her thumb along the surface and felt of the carved leaves and raised replica of a rose on the wooden handle.

Malachi looked at the men and back at the lady to answer her question. He could tell that she was very interested, and the men seemed intrigued with his comments.

"These were cheaply made for the average household. Only very wealthy families can afford the best silver. On this, the silver is very thin, a coating probably over copper, brass, or any surface to make it pretty and shiny." He didn't figure they'd understand the details of pouring and molding, so he refrained from further descriptions. He picked up the large spoon. "Look closely, and you'll see it's tarnished, hasn't been polished in a while. The agent at Denver City said that the Townsends left two years ago, so I guess it's been in the cabin that long. Even though it's not the best quality, it'll make a very nice piece of dinnerware once it's been cleaned and polished." He looked at the frock coat, whom Stockwell had called Hezekiah. The man turned to the woman and she nodded.

"We'll buy the spoons, knives and the large spoon from you, Clements, and the pewter plate. How much do you want for them?"

"Whatever the proprietor says is a fair price for the supplies I need in his store." He tossed the problem back in the lap of the man behind the counter. He might not want to barter for used merchandise, but it was clear to Malachi that he wanted to please the gentleman and lady.

"I'll agree to that, Mr. Clements. Just point out what you need. Is that agreeable to you, Hezekiah?" The frock coat looked at his lady again and she nodded.

"I suppose it's time we introduced ourselves to you. I'm Hezekiah Crandall, and this is my wife Betsy. We're from Connecticut, been here about two years. I'm a lawyer by trade. That gentleman is Thomas Surrell from Boston. He's a cobbler but doesn't have much call for shoes hereabouts. He has a claim about twenty miles from here on Fossil Creek."

Malachi was estimating how far it was to his first claim and figured that Surrell must be somewhere close to Potter's claim, which was supposed to be his. He was the man in the blue plaid shirt and didn't look like he knew anything about mining. Maybe that's why he hung around in Astra all the time. He was short and stout, with a gray beard and brown eyes. He couldn't tell the color of his hair because he had a flat-brimmed hat pulled low on his head.

Surrell picked up a covered basket of goods that he had apparently already selected before Malachi arrived and went out the door with a casual wave to everyone. Crandall and his wife followed him, taking the silver and pewter plate with them. They stood outside the building for a few minutes talking to Surrell, then separated and went on their way.

"I'm Moss Akins, the proprietor of the place.

You just select what you need, and I'll bag it for you." Mr. Akins was now all smiles and friendly complacency.

"I'll take the rest of your things, might see what some of the other miners need. I live in the log cabin near the stables. That's my business, livery horses and wagons. Come see me when you're finished here, and we'll talk." Stockwell helped Malachi put the other things back in the bag and hefted it over his own shoulder and left.

Knowing how much the silver plate was worth, Malachi selected a goodly amount of supplies, basic things that would keep him going for a few weeks, until he returned to the area. A bag of flour, one of corn meal, lard, salt, a slab of bacon, a string of Mexican red and green peppers for seasoning, several tins of peaches and canned milk, a dozen potatoes, a pound of coffee, dried beans and dried apples soon found their way into the mule's pack. He left the store pleased that he hadn't paid out any of his silver coins for the food supplies and had established a credit line for more supplies with the proprietor.

He untied the horse and mule and moved up the road to where he'd seen the livery stable when he first entered the town. He pulled up in front of a log corral with maybe a dozen horses and mules standing around and eating their daily rations. Stockwell met him at the door to a small log cabin.

"Come in. Come in, Clements. It isn't much to look at, but it kept me from freezing last winter."

He turned and went ahead into the one-room building. It was clean and warm, with a fire burning brightly in the fireplace. Malachi saw his burlap bag with the kitchen items lying near the table. "I don't have many visitors of your character. Most of the men are simple-minded farmers, down on their luck and trying to get rich quick. The most experienced miners have taken their share and left the area. I don't know why I stay; can't make any money here. No one wants to take a Sunday ride in a carriage, and the others have their own animals. Sit down. Sit down."

Stockwell went to the fireplace and pulled a blackened coffee pot from the coals. He set two tin cups on the table and poured some of the hot brew into each one. "Sorry the coffee's not fresh. I made it before I went to Akins' store. If you don't like the taste, just let it set." He sat in the chair and leaned his arms on the table. He took a sip of the coffee and sighed.

Malachi thought it only polite to drink the coffee, since he was here on a business deal. He liked the man. He seemed cordial and well educated. He hadn't made friends while in the Army and had lived alone for so long, maybe it would be good to sit and talk a while. He took a sip, and it wasn't bad. Not what you could call good but not bad. He took another sip before setting the cup aside.

"I suppose you don't want to leave your animals standing out in the cool air with the saddle and pack on, so I'll get straight to the point.

There's a lot of poor men here, some of them with wives and children. I try to help them when I can. A few farmers have some vegetable crops, and one of them, a man named Brady, has a field of oats. Now, I don't know whether I can get rid of those things for you, but it doesn't matter. I'll give you a five-pound bag of oats for them. That way it'll help Brady and you, too. On one condition, that is." Stockwell looked closely at Malachi and cleared his throat.

Malachi thought it a good bargain since the things weren't really worth much; it had been the silver that was valuable. A bag of oats would sure be worth the effort, so he agreed.

"What's your condition, Stockwell? I'm not staying here long; I have my other claims to work and have to get down the mountain soon."

"I won't keep you long. I'm just curious why a man like you with your skill and education would want to come so far from the big city to this out-of-the-way place. There must be something back in Springfield that would suit you better." Stockwell finished his coffee and waited for an answer.

Malachi wasn't sure he wanted to divulge his whole life story, so gave him a shortened version.

"I was drafted into the Army by Mr. Lincoln's orders so didn't have any choice in the matter. Besides, I have a younger brother, and I figured if I went, he wouldn't have to. He could claim to be the sole support of our parents, if something happened to me. As you can see, it did. Artillery shrapnel sliced my hand off. The doctors mended the veins and muscles, and I was in the hospital for several weeks recovering. A man in the bed next to me had a claim down the creek a ways, and he told me about this place. He talked about it all the time; the beautiful mountains, the bracing air, the huge boulders and the pine forests. I decided that I may as well come and see for myself, so here I am."

Malachi had stretched the truth a bit, for the man had never mentioned the place before that last night, but Stockwell wouldn't know that.

"What happened to the man?"

"He died."

"Oh." Stockwell frowned as if considering the matter, then his face brightened; and he waved his hand as if dismissing Malachi's answer as of no consequence.

"The agent at Denver City said there were three abandoned claims, so I took them all. It seemed that at least one might prove to be successful. If not, I have three homes, and if I decide to sell two of them, I'm still ahead. I'll never go back to Springfield. I'll tell you something else, Stockwell, if you'll keep it under your hat."

"I'm not one to talk about a man's secrets, but if you feel like you can't trust me, then I'll not keep you any longer." Stockwell looked like a spoiled boy, deprived of his favorite toy. It was clear he desperately wanted to hear Malachi's story.

"I don't mind telling you, but I haven't made up my mind yet what to do. That's why I said what I did about keeping it under your hat. I may just work my claims. Maybe, I'll strike it rich, who can say. But, you mentioned my education. I've been trained in geology and minerals and the mountain flora and fauna of the west. At least what the scholars know about it so far.

"The Rockies have a multitude of places that haven't been explored yet. I figure it like this: when the gold plays out, men will start looking for other things, like silver, copper, and precious jewels like rubies, diamonds, and emeralds. I might sell all my claims and become a hermit, wandering in the mountains and looking for the treasure I know is here, if a man just looks close enough. Mark my words, when this war's over, men'll be flocking west in great numbers looking for something besides gold."

"That's true, I'm sure, Clements. I don't know about those things you said, but I suspect the people of the East will have a belly full of war and desolation. They'll come to the mountains, alright. There might be stage coaches and railroads through the area in twenty years or so. I don't plan to stay that long, but a young man like you might make it if you stay. The gold's about gone; most of the farmers will starve if they don't get out and find better places to plow their fields and raise their families. You take that bag of oats, and good luck to you." Stockwell rose and went to the back of his shed where he lifted a bag of oats and brought it to Malachi, who followed him from the house and shifted the items in his pack to support the new weight.

"Thank you for the oats, and I hope you can find someone who can use the items in that bag." Malachi held out his hand as a means of concluding their business.

"You come back to see me when you're in the area, Clements. And, I won't tell a soul about your plans. It isn't any concern of mine, what a fellow does with his time." They shook, and Malachi mounted his horse and headed back down the trail to Fossil Creek. He felt guilty for telling about his dreams, but that's all they were, and if he didn't search for the minerals, someone else would, he was certain.

He reached his cabin well before dark, and after seeing to the animals, went to bed. The next morning he cached some of his durable goods and cleaned up the area. He left a sign on the cabin door like he had at the first one, proclaiming that he was the new owner of the claim. Early the next morning, he was on his way to the dugout claim where he stayed almost two weeks, not finding any trace of gold dust, then went to Brinkley's Manor. He stayed there for a month, but nothing as exciting as finding the silver coins happened there.

At each place, he bartered for goods until he had nothing else to sell. He became a familiar sight moving up and down the trail, riding his roan horse and leading the mule. He became known as the one-armed man with the pack mule. The miners eventually began to leave the area, looking for new diggings somewhere else. The abandoned claims were sold to farmers who tilled the soil and grew crops of wheat, barley, oats, corn and vegetables, which Malachi was pleased to buy to supplement his diet.

The village of Astra grew in size and stature. The early settlers moved on, and the farmers and merchants built schools, churches and an opera house. Jason Stockwell stayed one more year in the town before selling his property to a tall, burly man, who prospered in the business and served on the town council. Malachi was sad to see the livery man go, for he'd become his only true friend.

The winter snows came and melted. The spring rains brought out the wildflowers in the meadows, and as will happen, the warm rays of the sun caused men and women to forget the harsh storms of the winter. Malachi sold Brinkley's Manor and the dugout cabin, and moved permanently into the high cabin near the town, staying there only during the harsh winters. He never learned to row the canoe and sold it for fifty dollars to a merchant in Astra. He never developed an interest in hunting for wild game, but often sat on his mountain cabin porch and watched them feed and drink at the stream.

The first government mail service came to the

town, and with it news that the Congress had voted to provide pensions for soldiers wounded in the line of duty. Malachi received news that his brother had married and taken a partner into the business. He'd sent the half share of the business to a Denver City bank in Malachi's name as promised. They kept up a regular correspondence, and if Malachi mourned for his previous life as a master silversmith, he didn't admit it to anyone.

Malachi Clements now had a settled income and interest on his bank account. Every spring he headed out from his cabin on his new horse, a bay stallion, leading a donkey he'd won in a poker game and named Hannibal. None of Malachi's horses were ever named, other than the generic moniker Horse. He traveled into the valleys and the gullies, and among the huge boulders, woods and meadows. He climbed partway up the snow-covered mountain he'd seen from a distance, chipping away at the rocks and digging under the tree stumps. He didn't find the mother lode, nor did he find tracings of silver, but he found all that he needed to keep him warm and well-fed. He never married and lived out his days in his home high above the claim of Jethro Belton, the Rebel soldier, who'd given him the gold nugget. After about ten years in the mountains, Malachi took the nugget to Denver where he had a jeweler mount it on a golden chain and sent it to his brother for him to keep until his niece attained her majority.

He didn't tell his brother from whence the

nugget came, and the legend grew in the Clements family that he'd discovered gold in the mountains. If there was gold on the Belton-Potter claim, it was never found. James Potter and his wife raised a large family, and he operated a saw mill for the growing number of settlers along the creek.

Malachi did find gold under the beaver dam on his own claim. He found it one particle at a time until he had a small bag of gold dust. He took it to Denver and made arrangements for payments to be sent to his brother for his nephews' education. When he died at the age of seventy-four, there were five thousand dollars in his Denver bank account. His eldest nephew, Thomas Clements, went to the city to settle his estate and was told of his property near the town of Astra. He and his wife fell in love with the place, and the property remained in the family for generations.

Each succeeding generation sifted the soil and ran the sluice looking for gold dust. Some of them found it, and some did not.

A Reluctant Hero

— 1 —

SPRING 1865
Wilmington, North Carolina

The brilliant colors of the Stars and Strips snapped in the brisk breeze. The parade grounds stood starkly empty in the misty light of the breaking dawn. A scattering of wispy clouds painted the North Carolina sky, cast as if by a giant's hand onto a pond, the water smearing their outlines into indistinct and feathery shapes. A solid bank of clouds on the horizon lifted its shoulder, holding up the sun that peaked over its massive bulk. In the distance, the Cape Fear River churned with widely dispersed whitecaps. A flock of white-chested sea gulls whirred against the bucolic scene, revealing life in the quiet of the morning.

"Sir!"

Former Gunnery Sergeant Clive Montrose turned to see what the excitement was about, only to find a young corporal, probably no more than eighteen, facing him, his hand at his temple in a formal salute. Montrose glanced around to see who the boy might be saluting, as he tried to blink sleep out of his eyes.

"Sir!" the young corporal snapped again. His back was ramrod straight, and his blue uniform showed the ragged use it'd been through the past six months. One leg was stained, just above a tear at the knee. Blood, Montrose assumed. It was a stain that rarely came clean. The cuffs of his jacket were frayed, and oversized, the coat appeared to have once belonged to another man. The small hole in the chest, just over the heart, suggested this boy hadn't been inside when it was made. A larger man had probably died so this boy could have a uniform of his own, even if it wasn't the proper size.

Montrose noted the ragged cut of his hair jutting in disarray from underneath his cap. Brown, it matched his coloring, with his deep-toned skin and sunburn scattered across his face and down his neck. Even his hand, bright against his cap, was littered with red. His brown eyes were dark knots. Montrose turned away, trying to remember the color of his own. It'd been so long since he'd looked in a mirror. He hadn't shaved in days. Hadn't had the soap or a blade to do so, making do with bathing in the river, but that as seldom as possible, with the spring barely slipping away. Maybe supplies would arrive today via steamboat.

Now that the war was finally over, by God, he hoped so.

"Sir," yet a third time, the corporal dared. He spat out more words. "A message, Sir!" The boy dropped his arm, and he felt inside his jacket and pulled out a folded paper. He held it out. With his other hand, he swiped at his nose with the sleeve of his jacket and sniffled loudly.

Montrose snorted. "Who you talking to, boy? Nobody here but you and me, and I'm barely awake."

"Yes, sir, Lieutenant. I was told to bring this to you soon as you showed." The boy nodded at the paper, extending it a bit more. He looked as if he might topple over if he tried any harder.

"Lieutenant?" Montrose felt his brain break through the morning's fog with the icy clarity of the past months. The war had ripped the country apart, but more importantly, it had decimated his platoon. Men had died from cannon ball strikes, many in the field, even more screaming in their beds, arms and legs cut away to alleviate the brutality of gangrene, then likely as not dying anyway, their moans filling the infirmary with ghastly sounds of despair night after night. Men who had no experience had moved up the ladder because there was no one else, no one suited to do the job needed, but someone had to fill the vacancies. If they were lucky, Washington condoned the advancements, sending official paperwork via the post. Sometimes the officers didn't live long enough to receive their new orders, and someone else moved up to take their place. The blunders of inexperienced leaders were a curse of their own, killing additional men. At least the Union was still in one piece, even if more men had died than this country could afford.

Montrose felt of his uniform. He wasn't dressed as a lieutenant. His head clearing from the fog of sleep, he remembered his own advancement in the field. It had been at Fort Fisher, no more than thirty miles distant. He'd moved up the chain of promotion just like everyone else. He'd been a gunman, filling the mortars with powder and shot, then holding his ears when the gunpowder explosively ignited, sending death barreling through the skies toward an unseen enemy. Only when the black smoke cleared could they tell if they'd hit their target. Once the guns were adjusted for accuracy, then they'd do it all over again.

The mortars were silenced now, thank God, but skill at firing his guns wasn't why he'd advanced. It was the hard hit his platoon had taken in January while liberating the fort from Rebel hands; the pulling of injured men from the water; and the saving of lives despite the dangers to himself. He pushed those images away and turned to deal with the Marine still standing to his side.

"Let me have that, boy!" Montrose reached for the missive, noticing how the hairs on the back of his hand had grayed with the war. His hair and his beard were likely the same, streaked with gray, if he dared look. He broke the wax seal, snapping the bias relief of the United States Army in half and unfolding the dense stock. The words were written in thick ink, in a scrawling script, one Montrose readily recognized: Amos, his nephew, now a lieutenant in the Army, lifted in the ranks the same as he.

Dear Uncle,

Now that you have achieved the elevated rank of lieutenant, I have no trouble at all in getting my letters to you. It seems rather more difficult in getting yours to me, as none seem to show up from your illustrious pen. I know you must be busy with your new position, and it pains me to chide you so, but it's my only way to reassure myself you still live and breathe. I write to you of my younger brother. Chester has now achieved the glorious rank of sergeant major. At least you'd think it glorious by the excess of celebration that occurred last evening. His chums toasted him repeatedly at the tavern, seemingly forgetting the whys of his promotion. Alas, the foibles of youth. Men who are injured and die from improper sanitation are of little concern, because youth will live forever. I was the same once, and I suppose you, also, although I cannot picture you, Uncle, as a youth refusing to admit you might have a flaw or two. You would simply stamp your feet and bid your flaws gone, and they would flee at your command. I'm writing to inform you of the gossip in the air. It seems that now the war is concluded, there are serious discussions of an award coming your way for your acts of bravery last January. If so, Mother has determined to travel with me despite Father's objections, although at the snail's pace Washington moves, I doubt anyone should start packing anytime soon. Medals will have to be minted after our excellent Senators and their various committees sort out the schedule. Once this gets rolling (if it ever does), you can expect all Washington to arrive with numerous military brass, politicians and what not, all men of esteem and great importance. They will attempt to commandeer your attention, I'm certain, but I hope in my heart to see you at that time. Thank God this damnable war is over, and we can enjoy peace once again.

Your loving Nephew, Amos.

"Damn," Montrose muttered, as he folded the letter and held it at his side. "An award, with all its pomp and circumstance. It makes my stomach jump."

"Isn't that a good thing, Sir?"

"You're still here, Marine?" Montrose looked at him hard, seeing the smile on his face, and finding the boy too ebullient for such an early morning. "Don't you have toilet duties or something? Surely you can find some wood to cut or rabbits to skin. Get on about your day and leave me in peace."

He waved the missive at the boy, shooing him away. He was surprised when the youth simply stood at attention, and his smile grew wider.

"What, Corporal? You've nothing else to do today?"

"No, Sir. I've nothing else to do today."

"Hell and damnation, man. What *do* you do on this post?" He'd have this boy skinned and mounted if he didn't wipe that ridiculous smile from his face.

"As of this morning, I'm your aide, Sir. That's what I do, Sir, whatever you tell me to do, the sergeant major told me."

"My aide? What the hell do I need an aide for?" Montrose glared at the man. "You have a name, son?"

"Damned Fool, Sir." The grin was back.

"What did you call me?" Now Montrose was growing angry. Nobody called him a damned fool.

"That's my name, Sir." Still grinning.

"You're shaving close to your Adam's apple, young man. Surely you have a real name."

"Not for the past two weeks, Sir."

"Why the hell not?" That was the stupidest thing Montrose had ever heard.

"You said I was a damned fool for signing up

143

for the Marines, and when you wrote your memoirs, everyone'd know my damned fool name, 'cause you'd make sure you wrote it that way."

Montrose laughed. He remembered. The boy had stumbled over a coiled rope on the ship's deck, and he'd picked him up. He hadn't seen the boy since, but he remembered now. He thought he might like this kid. "You got any other names? Like the one your mother called you when you were a wee ankle biter?"

"If you don't mind, Sir, that one's sorta embarrassing. My pa called me Henry. My last name's Trotter. Will that do, Sir?"

"Trotter. I like that. Well, Corporal, it seems I may be attending an award ceremony before too many months are up. If so, your message says my sister's coming for a visit, also. Since you're mine, how 'bout we get some proper clothing lined up? I suspect this isn't correct duds for a lieutenant, is it, son?"

"No, Sir, I don't suppose so." Trotter pulled at his sleeves, as if trying to hide his own tattered and worn cuffs.

"You have any idea what I should have on? I'm a gunner, man. I've no clue."

Montrose sighed at the thought. His promotion had been a field advancement, one of necessity of the moment, with no uniforms, medals, or insignia to accompany it. He'd since received a formal communication from Washington, with mention of an upcoming citation. He supposed once the matter was decided, he'd be ordered to travel to New Orleans on the first available means of transportation. He'd rather have food for his men, ammunition for his guns, and shoes to replace those of his men's that had holes worn through the soles. If the brass were coming, however, they'd expect uniforms, so that he must have.

"So, Corporal, any ideas?"

"No, Sir, but I'm good at scrounging. You said it'll be several months?" The boy had pulled his cap off, and he held it in his hands, turning it around and around as he spoke. His hair caught the sunlight that was slowly overtaking the grounds, and it jutted every which way, even worse than Montrose had thought it might.

"I did, but no need in waiting. How about a week, maybe two? And this, on my shelf, please." Washington might move more quickly than expected, now that the war was concluded. His uniform had to be ready. Montrose held out the letter, waiting until the boy took it.

"A week's good, Sir, and two's better. We'll get you dressed. I can do that, Sir. I won't disappoint you."

"You're a damned fool if you do," Montrose snorted.

Trotter laughed. "I have been for two weeks, Sir. No reason to change that now."

Montrose laughed again. He knew he was going to like this boy.

"Dismissed, Corporal. I want breakfast at a quarter of."

"Sir!" and the boy was gone in a flurry of dust; leaving the lieutenant to warm his face in the rays of the rising sun.

— 2 —

Corporal Trotter, in his tattered uniform and ever-ebullient optimism, scurried about Montrose's quarters, laying out the morning's effects and straightening the things left from the night. A fine coating of sand lay across everything, and he brushed it aside. A week had passed, and he planned to see his superior outfitted with weapons before the day was done. When he threw back the shutters, he cried out, "Sir! The Good Lord's smiling on us today. Come see."

Impossible clouds streaked the morning skies. As the sun reached long fingers above the buildings of Wilmington, the wisps of feather-like clouds that oozed with wild abandon across the horizon burst into flame, shading the stucco walls with ocher shadows as if the gods of hell were passing overhead.

"Smiling?" Montrose growled. No morning was good, not by his standards, especially not before breakfast. He snapped his suspenders onto the waist of his pants, muttering quiet curses when he pinched his finger and had to undo the snap and start over.

"Yes, Sir. In bright orange, too. Come see." He stepped back to give Montrose a good view of the sunrise. The corporal's brown hair gleamed with reddish highlights in the orange hues. He blended into the ruddy shadows filling the room as he withdrew into the darkness.

"Come see, hell. I can't come see without my pants falling down. Get over here, Corporal. I need you." Montrose looked up to find the boy, his eyes just catching the multihued brilliance increasing its hold on the heavens. "Eh, boy, you say that's Our Lord? Seems rather devilish to me." He chuckled and, with a snap, got his suspenders attached.

"Perhaps, Sir. Still, it's pretty. Won't last, though. Already fading at the edges. Better look while you can."

It was something encouraging to see, Montrose had to admit. An auspicious start to what he hoped would be a fine day. Trotter had been good to his word and rooted out a warehouse that might provide a good saber and revolver, if the price were right. There were stories out there how prices seemed to mysteriously jump when a Marine uniform came a riding. Montrose wasn't having any of it.

"Son, what's my uniform for the day?" The

shipment had not yet arrived, and they had to make do as well as possible, even if sometimes they only had dead men's outfits to wear.

"How's this, Sir?" Trotter unrolled a uniform jacket in quite good shape, one that appeared clean. Montrose stepped to it, touching the shoulders and emblems, sighing when he realized it was a colonel's.

"Whose—" Montrose started, and cut himself off. Maybe it was best not to know. Rebel bands who hadn't accepted the end of the war had attacked the expected supply shipment, setting it afire in the river before it could reach the city. It was a time to make do with what they had.

"Can't say, Sir. So many—" Trotter looked to the floor, and he coughed respectfully. A slender youth, average in height, Montrose topped him by several inches, delineating their order of rank quite nicely. He looked up, speaking softly, "It could be anyone's, Sir. Sometimes they're buried with their clothes on, but the ones who die in the infirmary, well, no use in burying something we can use, if we've nothing else to replace it. Is that right, Sir?"

" 'Bout as right as tearing a nation apart by killing its best sons. This is a colonel's set, am I correct?"

"Yes, Sir, so's they said. That seems right to me. See, here." He ran his fingers over a place where an emblem had been removed. "It's not right for you, but it's the best I could scrounge on short notice. I'll have you done up right before your ceremony. You can count on me there, Lieutenant."

"Thank you, Trotter." Montrose turned to the window. As predicted, the reds and oranges had begun to fade. The walls of the station were again dun and dust, with bits of green along the base where men nor animal could get purchase to walk. The sounds and smells of the river reminded them how close they were to the shore. "Horses?" Montrose called, turning to look at his aide for his response.

"Coming, Sir. Jenkins, that's my friend in the stables, he's procured two fine animals for today. We'll be in style, Lieutenant, hand-tooled saddles and everything."

"And everything?" Montrose smiled.

"Yes, Sir. You won't be disappointed." Trotter noticed Montrose looking inside the jacket, and he stepped forward to lift it from the bed, holding it for his superior. "Sir, I believe we have time to get your breakfast before we head out, if you wish to finish dressing now."

"Breakfast. Yes, that sounds good. Then off for a good revolver and a saber for my belt. Thank you, Corporal. I'm lucky to have you at my side."

"Thank you, Sir." Once the jacket was firmly on, Trotter pulled a flat brush from his pocket and brushed the shoulders until no more dust flew free. Breakfast first, then to the stables, and the day could begin.

"Marine, ready for breakfast?" Montrose

nodded at him.

"Yes, Sir, always." The slender corporal grinned in anticipation.

"Then, man, let's do it." Montrose strode forward, walking alongside his aide towards the enlisted men's mess.

Inside the rough wooden building, large iron heaters sat in the middle of two long rows of tables. The heaters stood on iron legs and vented directly through the ceiling. Enameled plates already rested along each table, with tin cups for liquids. Piles of toasted bread, eggs, and sausages decorated the spread up and down the room. Milk was being poured into the cups by men in long gray aprons that hung nearly to their feet; their long shirt sleeves were rolled to the elbows.

Trotter made to step inside, but seeing Montrose hesitate, pulling a cigar aimlessly from his pocket, he waited to see if his superior needed anything more.

"Sir, not hungry today?" Trotter glanced inside at the sausages on the tables. A man who had arrived before them picked up one between his fingers and bit into the end. Juice ran down his chin, and he laughed, dabbing it with his finger. Trotter looked away when the lieutenant began to speak.

"Don't think this is right, Corporal Trotter; I ate with the officers yesterday."

"But, Sir, I seen you eat with the men plenty of times. Then, I guess with your new rank—" He shrugged. "Guess that's the way it is. Officers move up and get their own places. I understand, Sir." He looked inside the mess again. Indeed, all the men were privates and corporals with one lone sergeant sitting near the window, his chevrons visible in the sunlight. He had nothing but a tin cup in front of him. Montrose frowned and placed his cigar back in his pocket. Men were making their way into the room, and the space was filling up. The degree of dress from the men at the tables ranged from fully uniformed to those in more utilitarian clothing.

"Best you should go, Lieutenant, sir. I'll meet with you later."

Montrose, feeling out of place under the circumstances, withdrew and followed a couple of officers to the long, low building next door.

— 3 —

Dust stirred with every step of the horses'
hooves. Montrose held his reins loosely in one
hand, enjoying the warmth of the sun on his face.
He was tall, even afoot, and taller in the saddle.
With his black hair, gray eyes, and broad shoulders, he cut an imposing figure. His narrow hips
sat easily in the saddle, although his eyes seemed
ill-at-ease in the dead colonel's uniform and boots.
The repeated clop-clop of the animals stepping on
the packed earth road was pleasingly repetitive.
The sky had cleared, and black-winged birds
hovered in thermals in the distance. They were
away from the sea, and the humidity hadn't yet
risen to unbearable levels. It was a rather pleasant
sort of day, and he was in a generous mood.

He would be more generous when he'd procured his own weapons to add to his stolen uniform. It felt stolen to him, as it wasn't of the correct rank. He trusted others to be so unfamiliar as

not to notice or point out his uniform's deficiencies.

"Tell me, Marine, where do you come from? Where's your home?" Montrose looked at him, letting his body sway with his animal, as he waited on his reply. The youth was lagging, and he motioned him to ride faster.

"Ain't got no home, Sir." Trotter pressed his heels into the horse's flanks, clicking at him to speed up. He took a deep breath, as the animal began to trot.

Montrose slowed down and gazed at him quizzically. "No home? Where were you born?"

"Ohio, Sir. Father was hanged for horse thieving; mother ran off with his lawyer; left me with my granny." Both men drew their horses to a stop. The cutoff was just ahead, and the conversation was yet to be concluded. Trotter's animal kicked the soil with one hoof, raising a cloud of dust. Trotter laughed and shook his head. "But she died."

"Such happens. It's the way of life. What happened then?"

"County sent me to an orphanage. Soon's I was old enough, I joined the Marines, and here I am." Trotter grinned, but his eyes were tinged with red for the first time Montrose recalled. They sat for a minute without speaking, as their horses shifted their feet, occasionally snorting at the lack of action.

"Well, that's sad. How old are you, Corporal?"

"Near twenty-one, Sir, best anyone can tell from the records."

Twenty-one. Montrose had thought eighteen. That explained corporal and not private. It was a wonder he'd even been allowed to enlist, he looked so young.

One of the children in the distance had seen them and stood watching, his hand shading his eyes. Montrose urged his horse forward.

"Well, let's get on. We've been sighted, and they'll be wondering why we're loitering out here."

"Yes, Sir! I'm ready." Trotter was back to ebullience in full form. He kicked his horse, and it jerked forward, turning its head to find the source of the pain.

"Careful, Marine. Take care of your mount, and it'll take care of you." He spoke over his shoulder. "Farmer's name is Shannon, you say?"

"Yes, Sir, though I wasn't told his given name. Suppose Shannon could be it, but it didn't come across that way."

"That him?" They'd reached a stacked log fence, and in the distance a man was slopping several hogs in a tidy enclosure. A short space away, a woman was hanging out her wash. The high-pitched sounds of children's voices punctuated the silence, and looking, Montrose found several scattered around, two chasing each other around a fat tree.

"Suppose so, Sir. I've never met him, only

received advice that he might have the things we need. That's all, Sir."

They made their way towards the barn. The grounds were alive with activity, more so than had appeared from the road. They passed several trees, one the same as the children had chased around. It seemed to be a large white oak, and the leaves shuddered in a freshening breeze. The children were nowhere to be seen. The farmer was missing from the pig pen, but the wife was still at work, lifting clothes from a rough-woven rush basket to pin them on her clothesline. Her back was to them. At one point, she hefted a pole under the center of the line to elevate it further from the ground. Through the door of the barn, a Navy supply officer they hadn't seen earlier was overseeing the lifting of several boxes of supplies from a wagon to the interior of the building for storage. He turned at the sight of Montrose and Trotter. A dog sniffing at the wagon hiked its leg to relieve itself, and finished, it meandered over with an interested look on its face.

"Back, Sow Boy." The officer, a captain by his uniform, caught the animal with his foot, and he slunk away whining.

Montrose sat up straight in his saddle and saluted, and the captain sighed, saluting back. "Something I can do for you, Colonel?"

"Not colonel, Sir. I'm awaiting a proper uniform, and I apologize for this one. The rank is lieutenant. Need a revolver, Sir." Montrose caught sight of the men working in the barn, and at his words, everything went quiet, as they stopped their work to gaze at Montrose. He cleared his throat, at first unable to get his words out, then stronger as he continued, "My name's Clive Montrose, Sir. Never had a revolver before; experienced with a musket, though."

"Say, aren't you that Marine who led the charge at Fisher last January?" The captain scratched his head, pushing his cap to one side. "Thinking you looked pretty familiar. I was there myself. Man, you saved some lives that day."

Trotter blurted enthusiastically, "That's him, Sir. Could be whole Navy's coming to give him a medal."

"That so, Lieutenant?" The captain looked amused.

"Maybe not the whole Navy, Sir." Montrose grinned. He'd not expected to be recognized. "And it's only conjecture at this point. You know Washington's timetables. But if it does come about, certainly Lieutenant Fagan and maybe Admiral Porter himself, if he's got the time. 'Spect it'll be New Orleans way, if it happens."

"Well, Lord's sake." The captain then noticed his men had shuffled closer to hear the conversation. He barked out, "What do you sods think you're doing? This isn't no gossip session. Get yourselves back to work, unless you want to be here all night to make up for lost time." He shook his head dismissively. Shoving his pad under his arm, and putting his stub of pencil over his ear, he started toward the door. "Come inside, Marines. I'll see what I've got here. My men found several revolvers out on the battlefield; can't say if they work. May need a gunsmith to repair one or two. There's a good man in town named Whitaker, I've heard; knows about weapons."

The barn smelled of hay, that and pies that no man would want to eat. Also, machines and armaments, the things of war. The light was dim, from the open door and a loft open to the sunshine. The walls were rough and well-used, and hung with farm implements. There were many spots bare, those places telling of a war that had sapped the country, using but not replenishing supplies from up and down the continent. They moved to a large square table with several weapons laid out on a bed of sawdust.

"See what you think. Any of these catch your eye?" The captain crossed his arms and waited.

Montrose reached for one, turning it to catch the designs etched into the barrel. It gleamed, even in the darkness, but Trotter pointed out a different one.

"That's the one, Sir."

Montrose hefted it. He blew the dust off the barrel and looked at his aide skeptically. "You know this one?"

"Percussion cap revolver by Metropolitan. Probably just come from the factory."

Montrose traced the barrel with one thumb as

his aide spoke.

"Thought it was a Colt," the captain muttered.

"Same here. Corporal, you know this for certain?"

"Colt lost its East Armory to fire in '64. Couldn't keep up production. Metropolitan of New York started making copies. Called this one a Navy Percussion, if I'm correct, Sir." He grinned with his speech.

"Still say it's a Colt," the captain said. "See the scenes engraved on the barrel?"

Montrose turned it, going down the naval scenes with a nail. "Looks like a Colt to me, also. Corporal, what do you have to say?" He smiled, expecting something fanciful out of the man's mouth. He blew into the barrel before cocking the hammer back and gently releasing it.

"Right here." Trotter took the revolver and flipped it over, pointing out the Metropolitan Arms Company brand. "My commander in my last unit had one just like this. He bought it special order, Sir."

"I'll be damned." Montrose laughed, and he clapped Trotter on the shoulder. "You're an all right aide, my boy. What would I do without you?"

Montrose paid for the gun with a generous amount of Marine script, and he and the captain began to walk down the aisles of military materiel and damaged goods found on the battlefield. Several muskets were stacked in a corner, their barrels crossed and tied with cord. While the officers talked, Trotter began a curious inspection of the goods on his own. At one point, he picked up a pair of sabers, withdrawing one and flashing it in the air.

"Found something, Corporal?" Montrose excused himself and made his way to his aide.

"Your saber, Lieutenant. This looks like a good one. No rust." After a short demonstration revealing the youth's lack of skill, Montrose wrapped a deal for the saber, a leather holster for the revolver, and several rounds of ammunition. They left the warehouse, mounted their steeds, and headed towards the naval station, pleased to have their day's mission complete.

— 4 —

SIX MONTHS LATER
New Orleans

Lieutenant Montrose was aroused from a deep
sleep by the sound of a loud thump near his front
window. He recognized the sound of the woods-
man leaving his weekly supply of wood for the
officers' quarters. The only light filtered into the
room through a crack in the window. The barking
of a dog could be heard as the cart rumbled along
the pathway to the next officer's rooms. Nearby,
the familiar crow of a rooster gave him a feeling
of peaceful awareness. The war was behind him;
New Orleans was a fresh experience; and today
was a big day. He was to meet Captain George
Butler of the *Minnesota*, Lieutenant Fagan of the
Wabash, and several officers from the other ships
of war that had fought at Fort Fisher. He stretched
and yawned.

"Guess I ought to get out of bed," he said aloud into the silent room. He'd grown accustomed to talking to himself when he was alone. But, he was reluctant to leave the warmth of his cot. The smell of stale tobacco and candlewax sent his mind back to the events of the last days. He still couldn't believe that his sister was coming tomorrow on the noon train, joined by his eldest nephew. It'd been so long since he'd visited the large, white, columned house on the hill where his sister had presided over the afternoon tea. He wondered if her hair was still red or had it begun to show signs of gray. The rooster crowed again, and his memories from the past flew out of his mind. He slung the covers back and put his bare feet on the cold floor. He shivered at the touch of the winter-frosted wood.

"Damn. I forgot to wear my socks to bed. Damn, again."

He rubbed his arms as he stumbled to the table, found a tin of matches and lit the lamp. Its dim glow slowly grew as it chased the shadows from the room. He pulled on his dressing robe from the back of a chair and stretched to his greatest height. He yawned again and felt of his chin.

"Better shave first thing. The captain doesn't like scraggly beards on his men." He paused a moment. "Especially on a day like today."

He began to hum a tuneless melody, surprised at how good he felt. Mornings were not normally his thing. Then, he laughed at himself for talking aloud. "Getting to be an old squaw; too many lonely nights and lost dreams, I guess."

He walked into the next room, crossing the worn wooden floor with soles quickly numbed to the cold. He could still feel pain, he discovered, as he stumped his toe on a forgotten book on the floor and cursed at his clumsiness. At the door, he unhooked the latch and opened it a crack. The grounds and buildings were shrouded in fog. He moved to the wood pile, shared by his fellow officers; gathered a couple of pieces of kindling; and hurried back to the relative warmth of the building. A fire would soon warm things up. Taking the iron poker, he stoked the still-live coals and placed a couple of chunks of wood chips atop them. He found a sheet of old newsprint, crunched it into a ball and placed it carefully between a coal and the chips. Instantly, it blazed up, and he stepped back from the glare of the bright light. Satisfied that the fire would soon warm his room, he turned to the battered coffee pot that Trotter had foraged from the company warehouse.

He took a tin cup from the shelf above the table, dipped some water from the small barrel by the back door and poured it into the coffee pot, repeating the gesture until he had enough for himself and Trotter when he arrived. He reached for the bag of coffee grounds and paused as he heard the dog again.

"Sounds like he's caught a rat; or more likely one of the men sneaking into camp after a night in town." He laughed. He and his friends had done that before the war. He remembered the night he'd been caught with a wench from the local tavern. The sergeant had given him a lecture that had made his ears burn with shame. He shivered at the almost-forgotten memory. Things were different now, he thought; he was an officer, and his friends had been killed in the war.

He put the coffee pot at the side of the grate; close enough for it to cook, but out of the flame. He turned back to his bedroom and threw the covers over the bed, straightening the corners according to military regulations. He could smell the coffee brewing as he drew his new uniform from the makeshift closet nook, fashioned by a sheet with many small holes and slung over a cord stretched from the wall. He placed his polished boots on the floor and laid his saber and belt on the bed. With one finger, he caressed the lieutenant's bar and, angry with himself for dimming the brass shine, he used the tail of his wrap to remove his fingerprint.

The sound of men aroused from their slumber grew louder, and he heard a fellow officer step out of his door and gather wood in the damp fog. There was a loud, long curse, and the door slammed shut. Clive laughed and finished his coffee. He took the cup, sloshed some water around to cleanse the inside and slowly moved to the other room to shave and dress for the day.

— 5 —

Standing in the middle of his room, dressed in the proper uniform of a lieutenant in the United States Marines, with epaulettes on his shoulders and gold tassels encircling each one, Clive Montrose worked at one sleeve with a flat, horsehair brush, removing a small piece of lint. His hat was a jaunty affair, the brim lifted to touch the crown on one side, with feathers on the opposite side and crossed swords on the front. He wore a wide belt, with his saber at his hip, and his revolver opposite. His white gloves set off the Navy color in sharp contrast. At the morning bugle call to breakfast, he glanced around the room to see that it was clean and tidy, and opened the door. He almost bumped into Lieutenant Michael Beaumont coming from his own room.

"Good morning. Looks to be a fine day once the fog lifts."

Beaumont laughed. "Fine, even with the fog, I

seem to think."

"Oh? How's that?" Montrose had a bit of something in his stomach, butterflies, his nephew might say. His sister was coming tomorrow, and he hardly caught what Beaumont said.

"Ever been to the mountains? God smiles on the mornings, and the fog kisses the land with His breath, leaving a layer of moisture everywhere. My momma used to say fog's a blanket of love laid down by the Good Lord above."

"Is that so? Maybe my momma says the sun burns away the fog, because life's better when the sun shines in." Montrose looked for Trotter. The man hadn't shown, and that irritated him.

"Ah, don't be so morose. Once this ceremony's over, you'll feel better." Beaumont laughed and clapped him on the shoulder.

As the men turned to walk to the mess hall, Montrose heard a shout as Trotter came running from his own quarters across the parade ground.

"I found it, Sir!" He stopped abruptly when he saw Beaumont. " 'Scuse me, Sir." He stepped back and saluted.

Both men returned the salute, and Beaumont frowned. "Yes, Corporal. What did you find?"

Trotter looked from one to the other and saw Montrose nod his head. The corporal shuffled his feet, clearly embarrassed, then looked away and back to Montrose. However, his eyes twinkled.

"I found the snuff box, Lieutenant, sir."

"Montrose? Are you taking up the habit?"

Beaumont smiled. "Or is there a woman in your life? Maybe a marriage is forecast for your future."

Clive Montrose ignored Beaumont and replied to his aide, "Good man. Come along, or we'll be late to breakfast."

All three men swiveled as one and began to cross the parade ground toward the building where men in uniform were gathering for the early morning meal. As they walked along, Beaumont leaned in to him and whispered encouragingly, "Snuff box?"

"Later, Beaumont." Montrose put him off. They hadn't yet made it when the bugle began to sound, and the men stopped. The ritual of raising the flag over the parade ground was in progress, and they snapped to attention. The flag lifted skyward, lost in the fog, before breaking out in a bright burst of color as it approached the top of the pole. The ceremony reached its end, and the men parted to their separate units.

****

That evening Montrose met Trotter after dinner at the stables.

"You still have that snuff box?"

Trotter drew a small bag from his pocket and handed it to him. He said with awe in his voice, "The shopkeeper said it's from England."

He opened the bag and drew out the small box. It was an oblong, papier mache snuff container painted on top with cornflowers and foliage. He lifted the hinged top and sniffed. It had been used but would please Minerva immensely, he was certain. "Magnificent," he complimented his aide. "Absolutely beautiful."

"Your sister will enjoy it, Sir?" Trotter smiled hopefully.

"Oh, yes. She collects them for a hobby. I do believe this will soon be her favorite." Montrose took a moment to admire it and slipped the package in his pocket. "Thank you, Trotter. You've done well. Good night." He began to walk away, his boots kicking up bits of manure and straw as he went.

"Good night, Sir." And with a jaunty leap over a hay bale, the corporal headed for his bed.

****

Their heavy footsteps echoed in the nearly empty train station as Montrose and Trotter made their way to the ticket counter. Montrose noticed two Marines standing in the shadows, talking. They came to attention when they saw the lieutenant pass by but didn't salute, and he gave them a nod of the head. He stopped at the barred window and spoke to the attendant.

"Good day, sir. Is the train on time?"

The man had a thick beard and hard-rimmed glasses perched on his nose. He looked up and blinked at the uniformed men. The pile of papers in his hand fell to the desktop.

"Ah, yes, sir. Right on time." He looked over his shoulder as the telegraph keys began to click. "Pardon me, gotta answer that."

Montrose stepped back and took out his time piece. He glanced at it and frowned. They were early. The clatter of the telegraph continued, and he watched the frantic attendant write something on a pad.

"I don't suppose we have time for a cup of coffee. What do you think, Trotter?" He glanced around, and the two Marines were gone, to be replaced by a heavyset woman in wide skirts, a tall man and a small girl with her thumb in her mouth coming in the door.

"I don't think there's any eating places nearby, Sir. Didn't see any as we drove up to the station."

Montrose shrugged his shoulders. He watched the couple talking for a moment and turned back to the entrance. The collar of his new uniform felt tight around his neck. He rolled his finger underneath to loosen it and felt the nick on his face from his early morning shave. The bleeding had stopped, but it was still painful. He took a cigar from his pocket and lit it. The smell of tobacco rose in the air, and he coughed.

"Well, if that's the case, we'll go outside and wait."

"Yes, Sir."

They moved toward the door and stood back as two men entered. One was tall and pale-skinned; the other shorter and younger, with heavy features and a pockmarked complexion. Both were dressed in ill-fitting clothes, and neither looked well fed. He touched the brim of his hat and nodded. They passed by, and Montrose led Trotter out the door. He heard one of the men mutter as he passed them, "Damn Army carpetbaggers."

He caught his breath. He wanted to call attention to his Marine uniform. They weren't Army, he thought, but he kept his silence. He walked to the edge of the building and stood beside a railroad gurney piled high with baggage and boxes. The early fog had lifted, and it promised to be a nice, sunny day. He squinted at the brightness, after leaving the dimness of the station.

"I could use that cup of coffee myself, Lieutenant, sir," Trotter muttered. "Don't those men know the difference between Marine and Army uniforms?" He lifted his chest in pride over his own dark blue suit, and he looked down at his boots to make sure they still shined.

"Civilians see all uniforms as a threat, I guess, after the recent hostilities. Probably Confederate businessmen on their way north to St. Louis. I'd be resentful, too, if I'd lost my home and business. Pay them no mind." He tipped his hat to a woman passing on her way to the door, dressed in the fashionable skirts of the time, a parasol in her gloved hand. Walking behind her was a dark-skinned woman with her hair covered by a bright red scarf. He nodded to her, too, and received a timid smile. A crowd was beginning to gather at the terminal.

He heard the sound of activity and looked to the left. About fifty yards away, near a culvert beside the tracks, a wagon had stopped. From what Montrose could make out, it was two men, one in a tall top hat and the other with a cane striking out at a group of dark-skinned men who blocked their way. He'd seen such trouble before. Apparently, the blacks had come to the wagon, begging for food, and been assaulted by the whites who refused to give them even a few pennies. One large black man was defending himself from the blows of the cane with his arms, while a smaller man held the horse quiet. The former slaves growled and yelled at their angry tormenter, and a couple tried to pull the driver from the wagon. Trotter stepped forward as though to go toward them, but Montrose grabbed his arm and stopped him.

As he held his young aide fast, he saw some men in the uniform of the local mounted police race up on their horses, followed by several men marching with muskets in their arms. They started at the outskirts of the crowd to shove and move the black men away. The two on horseback reached the wagon through the melee and, with harsh words that Montrose couldn't hear, calmed the situation. The black men began to disburse and walk slowly back along the tracks, the armed men marching in step behind them. Montrose could now see, huddled under a tree, a group of women and children. He was too far away to see them clearly, but he knew from previous incidents that the women and children would likely be emaciated and poorly clothed.

He drew his attention back to the wagon and saw what looked to be the man in charge raise his arm in an authoritative gesture and point to the highway leading out of town. The driver of the vehicle turned the horse and drove away, a cloud of dust obscuring them from the sight of the two men watching from the station. The men on horseback followed the wagon until it disappeared.

"Don't seem right, somehow, Sir," Trotter growled from the side of his mouth.

Montrose was only half listening, as he heard a train horn in the distance. "What's that you said, Corporal? Never mind; the train's coming." His heartbeat picked up speed, and he took a long puff on his cigar to calm it. A few men had gathered near the tracks and looked toward the black smoke rising in the air.

"Yes, Sir, won't be long now." Trotter moved nearer to the tracks, but Montrose stayed where he was and finished his cigar. He didn't want the smell of tobacco to upset Minerva. He remembered her objection to his smoking in her house. He smiled and adjusted his wide belt, running his thumbs just underneath to flatten the fabric of his coat. He rubbed the palms of his gloves lightly against one another and stretched his fingers. Catching sight of his dusty boots, he lifted his left leg and shined his boot on the back of his trouser leg, then his right toe. An insect buzzed his head, and he swatted it away. He could feel the press of people as the crowd swarmed the tracks, waiting for passengers or ready to board.

A flash of memory crossed his thoughts as he remembered leaving his home in Virginia as a raw recruit, his parents and sister wishing him farewell. It seemed such a long time ago. The years had matured him, and he watched the excitement in Trotter's face as he anticipated the arrival of the behemoth, now puffing into the outskirts of town. The cry of a young girl distracted him, and he turned to see the couple from the earlier encounter in the station. The man picked her up, whispered something in her ear and she stopped crying.

A great sigh of relief filled the crowd as the train engine stopped a few yards from the entrance to the station, its smokestack bellowing black ash and smoke into the air. The sides gleamed with brass, highly polished in places, and in others, tarnished and blackened with soot. The brush guard at the front formed foreboding teeth, ready to reach out and grab unwary pedestrians. The engineers hunkered behind walls of glass, captured within the engine, as if unable to wrest their freedom from the beast. Trotter stood as though carved from stone, and Montrose called to him, but his voice couldn't be heard above the swell of voices. An attendant dressed in a black suit and white collar, his cap hoisted casually on his head as though it had been hastily pulled on, stepped down and pulled a step with him from the train. With a flourish of activity, the people circled the car door.

Montrose stood and watched as a man in battered hat and overalls stepped down, followed by another and another. There was a pause, and a slender man in the uniform of the Army appeared. He gazed around him at the crowd and stepped down, and then turned and held out his hand to help the woman who took his hand to follow.

Montrose felt his heart rise in his throat as he recognized his sister, dressed in dark purple with a hat of black felt and a ribbon of white atop her head. He tried to get closer but was stopped by the press of human flesh surrounding him. The woman was followed by a few more passengers, and they stepped to the side to give room, as the crush of bodies forced him to move away. He called out, "Amos!" but his voice wasn't heard above the din of activity.

"Amos!" he yelled louder. The tall, slender man turned and looked around. Montrose waved his handkerchief in the air, and with a grin, Amos Southerland whispered to his mother, and they walked toward the station.

Out of the corner of his eye, Montrose saw Trotter move from the crowd and walk toward him. Again, the wail of a young girl caught his attention, and he saw the girl from earlier being carried on her father's shoulder as they prepared to board the train. He turned his attention to the woman in purple. His heart thumped madly, and his face broke into a huge smile. But, before he could greet her, he was saluted by the younger man, and he had to respond. He wasn't sure of the proper protocol between Marine lieutenants and Army lieutenants of the same rank. He hadn't read anything about it in his book of instructions, and in the moment, he froze.

"Well, that's enough of that, Brother." The woman huffed as she broke the silence that had come over the men. Her gray eyes twinkled, and her teeth shone white between ruby lips. Dangling from one wrist by a chain handle was a small cloth handbag. Her bosom heaved with excitement, and Montrose could see the wrinkles near her eyes. She turned to the shy corporal standing with his jaw open in awe at the events unfolding before his eyes.

"You, there. Go see about my baggage. And, be careful of my hatbox. I bought a special bonnet for the occasion, and I don't want it crushed." She gave Trotter a frown and handed him a ticket to identify her luggage.

"Yes, ma'am, Sirs," and Trotter took the ticket and left to do her will.

"Good man," Montrose heard Minerva Southerland say, before he was folded into the embrace of his sister, not caring of his uniform or his rank or height.

"Clive." That's all she said, and the lieutenant

felt the tears sting his eyes. He could smell the vanilla in her hair and tried to step back, but she wouldn't let go of him.

"Minerva, it's good to see you, but it's not at all the thing for a lady of your position to hold onto a man on the platform of a train station," he admonished her.

Startled at the scolding, she stepped back and began to laugh. The hat on top of her head started to tilt to the side, and she grabbed it in time. She looked at Amos and straightened her shoulders, letting her arms drop to her sides. Montrose could see a faint pink tinge on her cheeks, and he felt compassion for her.

"I have a buggy waiting. I've reserved a room in a local hotel of good reputation for you and Amos, if you'll follow me." He held her by the elbow as he led her away from the few remaining stragglers standing by the train station and onto the grassy verge where a buggy and horse stood by.

"Thank you, Clive. What a dear you are." She smiled as she gathered her skirt in her hand, watching for possible obstructions as she crossed the grass. Her black and saddle shoes, quite elaborately worked and laced to her ankles, appeared from time to time underneath her cotton twill skirt over crinoline. Her matching jacket had a bolero-style front with split sleeves. Her white Garibaldi blouse sported mother-of-pearl buttons down the front.

"Was your trip pleasant? I know the tracks

aren't as smooth as they should be, but with the war, you know, maintenance was kept to a minimum as the men left for the North." He stopped as he watched Trotter come up, carrying a multi-colored carpetbag and a hatbox. In his other hand he held a large brown satchel. Amos reached to take it from him and lifted it into the back of the buggy. Together they tied the luggage to the vehicle.

"It was pleasant enough, although I thought we'd be wrecked when we crossed over the river, the current was so swift. The framework of the trestle moaned like a ghost of the past as we crept across it. I glanced down at the raging water and held my breath, but we had no trouble."

"Mother thought we might fall in," Amos teased.

"Was the bridge not sturdy?" Montrose caught his nephew's tone, and he ribbed his sister, also. "I suppose it's happened before, for a bridge to just collapse of no accord."

"You men, always making light of women's fears. You should be ashamed. The water was quite fierce, creating magnificent sprays all around the trestles." She wore a smile as she said it, however. "One thing that truly showed me the war has had a terrible effect on people across our country was those on foot. I never saw such a large group of dark-skinned people moving toward the North. The train had to slow down several times because of them. We saw campfires beside the tracks at night. Amos said they were stragglers, homeless men, women and children trying to escape the desolation. Now that the President has set them free, they don't know where to go."

Montrose helped her into the seat and patted her arm. "That's true. We've long lines in the city, with people begging for food and camped in the open parks. But, you don't need to worry about that now. You're safe with the military all around the city. Now, Amos, you wrote about your brother in your letter. Have you heard from Chester since?" He took his seat in the back row, as Amos climbed up beside him, and Trotter untied the horse and stepped into the driver's seat.

"Ha, Uncle." Amos laughed. "Ches is the perfect officer. The war is over, and he can parade about in uniform at all the dances, and every girl wants to be his partner. He loves military life, as would I, if mine were so easy as his."

"Amos!" Minerva turned to him and wagged her finger. "Chester is just a boy. You be kind when you speak about him."

"It's Uncle, Mother. He knows Ches, and he won't be surprised at his womanizing."

"Harrumph!" Minerva turned to the front, clearly exasperated by her son's forwardness.

"Francis, is he doing well?" Montrose directed his question to Amos. "Your father is one who benefited from the war, even as he aided the war effort. How are his business interests faring?"

"Papa has his fist on all matters financial. A

dollar doesn't dare escape his pocket, if Papa doesn't give it permission now that the war is over and the shop is open once more. Isn't that so, Mother?"

"He was generous with your passage on the train." Minerva lifted her nose. "It's Chester I wish to talk about. Clive, you must assure me you'll make the greatest effort to rein your younger nephew in. I'm afraid he'll become a dandy if not assigned some duty in the western territories."

"Ha, Sister." Montrose felt a laugh rise in him, and he fought it. "My new rank is a field advancement only. No one'll listen to me where it concerns Chester. I'm afraid he'll have to work his own way through his peacetime cotillions."

"Well said, Uncle." Amos nodded agreeably.

Montrose laughed, and he looked around him as they moved toward the hotel, trying to see the scene as a genteel lady would, focused on the many men standing and sitting near the buildings, with no purpose since the war was over.

A few mounted policemen patrolled the streets, and armed men stood in clusters at the intersection, ready for trouble. After the scene he and Trotter had just witnessed, he was grateful for their presence.

The vehicle stopped in front of the Royal Pavilion Hotel, and Montrose stepped down from the seat. The extravagant building towered over him for three stories. Black shutters framed the windows, and far above them, gracing the top, was an elaborate cornice piece of painted iron. The portico along the street shadowed a dozen columns of fluted iron, done in glossy green paint to complement the sparkling cut-glass door. He held out his arm for his sister, who graciously took it and joined him on the dirt street. A few steps took them to the door of the hotel, and he held the door for her. Amos took the luggage from the buggy, setting it on the ground at his feet. Trotter, seeing everyone was clear, snapped the reins and headed to the livery stable.

The lobby was filled with visitors, men in uniform and in dark civilian suits, accompanied by women in voluminous skirted dresses of many colors. The interior was heavy with dark woodwork, including an ostentatious staircase leading to a wide landing halfway to the second floor. Just above it was a tall, stained-glass window depicting three angels hovering over Moses in the rushes. The ceiling far overhead was coffered and silvered, and it shimmered in the light of numerous oil lamps. Overstuffed velvet chairs with ornate frames filled every nook and cranny, and velvet wallpaper in a green paisley pattern covered the walls from a wide chair railing upward. He led Minerva to the counter where a harassed-looking man was talking to a short, dumpy fellow in a checked coat and dark trousers. He held a sheaf of papers in one hand, and his cane hung over the other arm.

"But, I have important business in St. Louis

next Friday. I need a room until my boat leaves on the morrow. Don't you have anything available?" The man's face was red, and a vein stood out on his forehead as he puffed and complained.

"No, I'm sorry, sir. We're full up. It's the same reason why so many people are in town. They're waiting for steamboats to take them upriver, or the train to take them to the East. You might try the Majestic Hotel down the street; it's larger and quite comfortable. Has a restaurant nearby, too."

"Larger, you say? Well, I guess I'll take a look." The man stuffed his papers in the pocket of his vest and stepped back. Montrose could see a silver watch fob on his chest as he turned. Minerva made a sound, and he looked at her curiously, but she was turned to the side of the room where a group of religious women were chatting like a string of birds on a tree limb.

"What is it, Sister?" He could see nothing amiss.

She shook her head, and the hat on her head tipped to the side. She reached up to right it.

"They were on the train in the same car. I spoke to the matron, and she said their convent was burned by a band of heavily armed Confederates. They stole all their food stores, leaving them with nothing, not even a roof over their heads. Horrible business. They plan to stay in New Orleans until contacted by their superiors in New York. I offered some money, but she wouldn't take it. Said the Lord would take care of them."

Montrose turned to look at the women again. He would like to help, too, but was certain they wouldn't accept it. He sighed.

"Yes, sir. Can I help you, Lieutenant?" the kindly clerk asked, and Montrose turned his attention back to the counter.

"I have reservations for my sister and nephew. The name's Montrose. They're staying two nights."

The clerk looked at the register in front of him, ran his finger down a column and smiled.

"Yes, sir. Rooms 207 and 208. That'll be six dollars, sir. Cash, you understand; we don't take Confederate money." His face was beaming, and Montrose wondered what was making him so pleased. He pulled out his wallet, removed the amount stated and handed it to the clerk. He shrugged. Must be the uniforms, he thought to himself.

Amos set the luggage on the floor and wrote his name in the ledger with a flourish, and the clerk handed him two keys and rang the bell. A slender young man came forward and picked up the heavier carpetbag, leaving the satchel and hatbox for Amos.

"Well, Minerva. I'll leave you to freshen up a bit. Take your time. I'll be back in a couple of hours for dinner. Is there anything you need before I leave?"

"No, I'm sure we'll be fine. Thank you, and I'll see you later." She moved away, her skirts swishing across the floor. She reminded him of a sailboat in the harbor.

"Don't worry, Uncle. I have the situation in hand." Amos grinned and shook hands. As Montrose watched them cross to the stairway, he glanced again at the women in religious garb, standing near a potted plant in the corner, quietly talking. He shrugged his shoulders and left the building. He stood for a moment under the porch roof and looked for Trotter. He took out a cigar and lit it.

"Oh, my," he said aloud. There was Trotter coming down the street with a young Marine private. They were talking animatedly, and Montrose was sure it was trouble on the way. But, the two men stopped and saluted smartly. He returned their salute and raised a brow in question.

"It's Private Goines, Sir. We heard the *Starlight* is about to chug up the Mississippi, and we want your permission to go watch. It's the very latest in steamboats, we heard."

"Rear wheel or side wheel?" Montrose remembered something of the ship being in port, but he hadn't seen it so didn't know the type.

"Side wheel, Sir," Goines replied with a broad smile. "With three decks and a stack as tall as a house."

"Corporal, you've seen this?" It wouldn't do for his aide to be led astray by this other man. He hadn't seen Trotter be untoward in any manner, and with his sister here, now was not the time for

183

it to begin.

"Only a glance, Sir, but it's magnificent. It puts out smoke near as much as a train. Sounds about like one, also. I should be pleased to pay careful attention and describe it in detail upon my return."

Montrose laughed aloud at the youth's exuberance. "Splendid idea. Take the whole afternoon. I won't need your assistance since I'll be visiting with my sister and nephew this evening. I'll tell the gunnery sergeant where you are, so he won't write you down as missing. Enjoy yourself."

He grinned at the enthusiasm of the men. He would like to see the ship leave port, too, but he had things to do before he came back to town. He enjoyed watching the ships enter and leave the harbor, but especially the sailing ships. There was something thrilling about the way the gray sails billowed in the wind that set him to thinking that he'd like to go to sea on a long voyage; as a passenger, of course, not as a worker. He chuckled under his breath.

He turned to the left and entered the Emporium, a building of two stories with a broad banner across the top advertising its wares, where he purchased some tooth powder and shoe blacking. His mind returned to the disturbing scene at the railroad tracks as he walked to the station and his duties.

— 6 —

Lieutenant Clive Montrose, his uniform freshly brushed and his boots newly polished, although dusty from his walk to town, opened the door to the hotel at precisely seven of the clock. He heard the large brass clock on the wall chime the hour as he crossed to the counter. He was very pleased with his timing, and he looked about. The lobby was filled with people, but he didn't see Minerva or Amos. He glanced up the stairs. Maybe he should go to his nephew's room. He started up the stairs when he was accosted by a burly, clean-shaven man with a brown felt hat crammed on his long brown locks. His breath was coming in gasps from his race across the room to see the Marine.

"Yes? May I help you?" He stepped back and turned.

"I asked the clerk, and he said you was the man who's being given a medal tomorrow for bravery, sir. Name's Abbott, sir. I'm with the New Orleans Inquirer; a reporter, you see? It's a small paper, but it's popular with the local workers. Could you give me a minute of your time, please? It's not often we get a celebrity such as yourself hereabouts. Get lots of politicians and plutocrats, but a real hero, that's something that needs to be in print, don't you think, sir?" The man's eyes sparkled with enthusiasm, and Montrose noticed the frayed edge of the man's suit collar as he swallowed.

"I'm not much of a hero, just happened to be in the right place when I was needed. You want a hero for your paper, go find Sergeant O'Malley. Now, he was the real hero; saved numerous lives, I heard tell. I was kind of busy at the time, you see."

"Yes, sir, but my editor said you jumped in the water and pulled plenty of men to safety, without a thought to your own danger. Must have been mighty bad, all the fire and hot oil and smoke around you. Can't you give me a few minutes? I'd be eternally grateful, sir."

"Well, I'm here to take my sister to the restaurant for dinner. And, my nephew. I don't have the time to spare. I'll tell you what I'll do. You come to the show tomorrow, and if I have time after the ceremony, I'll sit with you for a while. But, I feel you'd be wasting your time. I'm not a hero. Just doing my job." He sensed the need in the young reporter, and he supposed the story should be best told by the person who lived it, but he was embarrassed to think it was him.

"Oh, very good, sir. I'll see if my editor will agree. After all, it might be better to write after the medal is given. That way, I can tell about the admiral coming and the colors of the flag and the band playing and everything. Make a longer column, it would. Maybe, I'll even get a raise in pay," he said hopefully with a grin.

Montrose smiled back. He couldn't help but like the young man, so eager and needful. He watched as the man withdrew and turned back to the stairs. But, he didn't have to go up, as he saw a lovely lady coming down, dressed in a pale cream dress and shawl. His nephew walked a few steps behind, his Army cap slightly awry, as though he had hastily placed it on his head.

"Minerva, my dear. You look lovely tonight. I'll be the talk of the town, escorting the most distinguished lady in the restaurant." He took her arm gently as she drew beside him, and they moved across the lobby floor towards the open door.

"Oh, go on, Clive. Your fancy talk doesn't make me think any the better of you. You'll always be my favorite brother, whether you're a smooth talker or not." She smiled.

"He's your only brother, Mother," came a sharp retort from behind. "But, he's right. You do look fine tonight. I wish Father could see you. He'd be pleased to know you experienced no ill effects from the journey south. It appears to be a pleasant night." He dropped back to let the couple talk as they walked the short distance to the restaurant.

"I chose this particular dining establishment because of the reputation it's received from the locals. The food's plain, but well cooked, and the service is excellent. I've only eaten here a few times but found it to be worth the effort. My neighbor, Lieutenant Michael Beaumont, raves about the lamb chops. Of course, with the visitors in town, it's bound to be busier than usual."

There were lampposts along the sidewalk, with large, fat candles inside. They cast just enough light for the trio to find their way in the gathering dusk. The building was a one-level affair, with a wide portico supported by simple wooden posts. Double doors were open, with large screened doors allowing the night air in. The interior was well lighted, with tables set for service just beyond the spacious entry hall. It wasn't a location to tease with substance and style, rather one that carried its reputation by service and function.

They were met by the maître d'hôtel, dressed in sober black, his hair slicked down with an oily substance. He held several large menus in his hand and bowed low when he heard the name of the man who had made the reservations. High overhead, crystal chandeliers gleamed and sparkled. The smell of freshly cooked meat permeated the room, and Montrose smiled in anticipation.

They were led to a table near the center of the room, and Montrose was pleased to see that several ladies were present. He'd feared that it would be mostly men, whether military or civilian. He noticed some heads nodding and a whisper of recognition as he passed the other tables. Oh, damn, he thought. He'd hoped no one would notice him tonight. Tomorrow would be bad if the word was already out about the ceremony at the station. He saw some officers that he knew at a table nearby and recognized his neighbor, Lieutenant Beaumont, and a couple of others from the officers' mess hall. He could feel his ears turn warm from embarrassment. He nodded and seated his guests.

Minerva sank gracefully into a seat and draped her shawl more comfortably over her shoulders. She opened her handbag and drew out a pair of spectacles from a leather case. She looked up in time to see the smile on her brother's face. "Hah, don't laugh, Brother. Francis says they're attractive, so I don't mind using them in public."

"And, how is husband Francis, my dear?" He was interrupted by a quiet voice at his side.

"Can I be of assistance, sir?"

"Two menus," Montrose requested. "One for my nephew, and another for me."

"Certainly, sir." The maître d'hôtel offered each of the men one of his menus, together with a sheaf of papers bound in bright red velvet for the wine, and disappeared to help other diners.

Minerva glanced up. When no menu came her way, she removed her gloves and sat rather stiffly in her seat as a waiter joined them, announcing his name, and that he would be their server for the evening. The men began to order for her, each competing for the honor.

"Oh, botheration, Amos. Leave it be; I can read the menu." She reached her hand to take the menu from her son and quickly lowered her voice when she noticed a stir at the next table. A well-dressed couple were quietly arguing, the woman turning to stare at their table, and the husband attempting to divert her attention to her own meal.

"Ignore them, Sister. I seem to be more of a celebrity than I might wish tonight. Tell me of Francis." Montrose gently touched her wrist before returning his hand to his lap.

Minerva took a sip of water and peered at her family over the rim of her spectacles. "Francis is just fine, as long as he smokes his cigars outside the house," she announced to the men.

Amos laughed aloud.

"Father burned a small hole in the arm of his chair one night when he fell asleep," he leaned over and whispered to Montrose, who lifted one eyebrow at his sister.

She sighed. "Yes, he fell asleep reading a book. I've warned him to be more cautious. Now, Amos, you mustn't tell tales of your father while we're visiting with Clive. The dear one is so proud of his business. Just think, he's once more been able to open the shop since the hostilities have ended. It was most depressing to see him struggle to keep going during the war." She was interrupted by a feminine voice, and turned to see who had come to their table.

"I say, sir. Aren't you the sergeant who was raised in rank because of your valor at Fort Fisher? I read about it in the St. Louis paper, about how you jumped into the fire and water to save those poor Marines from drowning. Is this your wife? How do you do, ma'am. You must be very proud of your man."

The speaker was the elaborately dressed woman of great style from the table next to them. Her dress was a red silk affair topped with a green velvet jacket, and her hair was coiled at the sides of her face and laced with green ribbon. Large bows in a matching green color decorated the front of her skirt. Her sleeves were pillowed in gathered rings that flowed to her wrists. She seemed to have appeared from nowhere as the three family members gaped at her in surprise at her audacity. A tall, spare man stood behind her and tried to lead her away.

Montrose rose slowly. He felt his legs quiver and his heart began to quicken.

"Ah, yes, I'm Lieutenant Clive Montrose. How do you do? This is my sister, Mrs. Minerva Southerland, and her son, Amos. Did you say you've recently been in St. Louis? Are you making a long stay in New Orleans?" He tried to change the subject, but he could see the other diners were listening, so he raised his voice. "You'll find our city a sharp change from the hustle and bustle of the city to the north. I hope you enjoy your stay. If you'll excuse me, my guests are anxious to begin their meal." He smiled.

"Come, Maud. I told you the man didn't want you interrupting his evening." The man held her arm tightly. Montrose could see he was upset.

"But, Augustus—"

"Excuse us, sir. We'll be going now." And he nearly dragged the woman away. The diners turned their heads to follow them from the room. Montrose sat down as the whispers continued around him.

The waiter stood silently by, his pencil in his hand and pad in the other. He cleared his throat.

Amos quietly ordered their meal and placed his snow-white napkin on his lap. He reached for a sip of water. "If this is a sample of the future, I'm glad I didn't win a medal for bravery in battle. I wonder if Sergeant O'Malley is suffering from the same notoriety."

"God, I hope not," replied his uncle with a sigh.

— 7 —

Montrose wondered where his aide Trotter had gone. He'd come by his quarters to help him dress and then disappeared muttering words about the need to see Private Masterson about something. He hadn't seen him since. He'd called on his sister and nephew at the hotel and driven them to the station, where he left them to find his place with his men. He looked up as a bird circled in the sky; he wished he could fly high above the parade ground. His hands were sweating and his knees promised to fold under him, as he awaited the part of the ceremony where he would march forward with Sergeant O'Malley to receive their medals. He hadn't had a chance to compare experiences with him, and he would like to have had the time to do so. He understood that O'Malley would take the steamboat after the ceremony to St. Louis where he would then make his way to the New York Naval Yard to continue his service to his country.

The sound of the admiral's voice made him impatient. Would the man never let go his speech? He only understood half the words, he was so nervous. All the men in uniform were standing still and quiet behind him, and somewhere in the crowd his family waited for the moment. Suddenly, he heard a drum roll, and the band began to play loudly. He came to attention as the moment he'd dreaded arrived. He nodded at O'Malley and marched forward to take his place beside him. The admiral stepped forward, and the two men saluted. Everything was deathly still as the admiral read O'Malley's citation and placed the leather-covered document on the table beside him.

O'Malley saluted and stepped back. It was his turn. Montrose thought he would faint. His throat was dry, and he swallowed; his heart thumped, and his ears felt full of cotton as the admiral read his citation. He blinked in the hot sunlight.

In the admiral's words, Montrose heard more, saw that day as though he were there still, the fort built of earth and sand construction and filled with the smoke of war rising in the distance, terrible with the sounds of death drifting across the water along the Cape Fear River. He could see abandoned cotton and tobacco ships that once would have departed for Bermuda lined along the shore, silhouetted against the silver-hued clouds barely seen through the hazy sky. The air was dense with smoke and fog, and the red death of leaping mortars decorated the heavens, as a heavy projectile hit the boiler of a gunboat and it caught fire. He glanced behind him, caught the pale shadow of his own ship and said a prayer for the men aboard.

The fog from his breath was warm against his wet cheeks, and he shivered in the cool air, made colder by his damp uniform as he tucked his body against the sandy soil. His ears rang with the shots of artillery and mortars. The sailors leading the charge were being felled like cut logs. Some began to run for shelter in a determination to save their lives. On the opposite shore of a shallow stream, Confederates armed with cutlasses clambered down the bank, screaming a victory chant as they leapt at the fallen men caught in the crossfire. As a Marine collapsed to his death, tumbling down a rise a few yards in front of him, Montrose rose and urged the men on, charging to the defense of his comrades. He raised his head in time to see an officer fall to the ground near the riverbank. That's when he saw the floating logs in the water, the blackened shapes that weren't logs at all.

Montrose was forced to make an impossible decision, take down the sour cad of a Southern rebel who had killed the officer, or aid the helpless men in the water, flailing their arms as they struggled to flee their attackers. In that moment of fear and danger, he knew the right choice, and taking a deep breath, he leaped from the shoreline into the water. It was cold, and he gasped with the shock as he fought his way to the surface, looking around wildly for the men he hoped to save. He gathered his wits about him and grasped for an arm, rolling one man to his back and lifting his chin. Breathe, man, he yelled. When water expelled from the vacuous lips, he knew there was a chance, and he was filled with a sense of power he hadn't known before. Wrapping his arm across the man's chest, he pulled by means of his swimming ability to a flattened section of shattered wood nearby. Looking for the second man who'd been floating alongside, he was relieved to see another Marine he knew only by sight, O'Malley, dragging the man to the far bank of the river before swimming back for more fallen comrades.

When Montrose's man began to cough, he was distracted from the other activity and turned him to his side until he could catch his breath. Ripping his own shirttail, he wrapped the man's injured arm as best he could. A splash at his side caused him to look, to find it was a Confederate coloring the water around him red. He was filled with pride at the fearlessness of his fellow Marines as they charged up the rise in aid of the sailors stealthily creeping near the fort's palisades. Swarming here and there were the uniforms of Union soldiers, sailors and Marines, joined in a common cause.

He hefted the man onto his strong shoulders and reluctantly turned his back on the scene of battle, carrying the man to the safety of a cart parked near the edge of the sea. Men, tired, bloody and dressed in rags helped him push the cart to the hastily built medical facilities where corpsmen in white coats red with blood awaited the wounded. Before the battle was through, Montrose ferried many more men to safety, numerous times dodging falling shells to rescue his injured fellows.

Finally exhausted, Montrose heard his fellow Northern Atlantic Blockade Squadron standing at the rails of his ship, cheering for victory and calling for Montrose to pay attention, as they helped him climb the rope ladder to the deck. Later, he learned through a Navy corpsman that many of the men he rescued were transferred to a nearby civilian hospital, and he almost forgot the matter, until he received the notification at his quarters in North Carolina of the award to be given him.

The admiral's voice stopped, and he stepped forward and saluted.

"Lieutenant Clive Montrose, it gives me great honor to bestow on you the highest award our country gives to those brave and honest men who serve her when called to duty with no thought to their own self-interest. On behalf of a grateful nation, Sir, I thank you."

Montrose looked straight ahead as he felt the slight tug to his uniform as the admiral pinned the medal to his chest. He stepped back and saw a tear in the admiral's eye and was surprised. He saluted, and a great cheer arose from the crowd as the band played, and he and O'Malley marched back to their places in the line of Marines. He felt relief wash over him as the ceremony ended with the playing of the band as the military marched off the field.

He had one short moment to congratulate Sergeant O'Malley before he was hauled into the embrace of strangers, clapped on the back and saluted by the members of his platoon. Somehow he made his way to his sister's side. She stood out in the gathering, a woman of exquisite taste, in her Zouave Imperial jacket, dark gray and untrimmed, reflecting the formality of the day, over a yellow blouse. Her parasol sported yellow tassels nearly the exact match of her blouse, and beneath her dark gray skirt, her shoes were trimmed in the same vibrant color. White gloves covered her hands, matching the ribbon jauntily jutting from the brim of her fashionable hat. She greeted him with a smile of pride, and he felt the sting of tears in his eyes. Amos stood stiffly by and waited before saluting.

"I'm very happy to be a part of your family, Sir. I hope I may be equally as courageous if called upon in my duties to serve." Amos grinned. "Could we eat now, Uncle? I'm starving." Montrose laughed, and suddenly there was Trotter by his side with his friend and several other members of his platoon.

"Sir, my friends and I would like to speak to you, if you please." To a man, their faces were sober, and Montrose wondered what was happening.

"Of course, Corporal, what is it?"

"Sir, we tried to think of something to show our appreciation that you're our commander, what with your new medal and all, but Sanstrom there said you wouldn't want anything for yourself, so we came upon a solution to our problem. With your permission, Sir." He turned from Montrose and spoke to Minerva.

"Mrs. Southerland, ma'am. The lieutenant told us of your snuff box collection. Now, I know he done gave you his gift, 'cause he told me you were pleased." He held out a small package, wrapped in white paper with a pink ribbon. "For you, ma'am."

Minerva took the package in her hand and slowly unwrapped it. Montrose could see that she was trembling. She lifted the lid and exclaimed at the contents. She removed the gift from the wrappings. It was a plain, lacquered snuff box, adorned with red roses and a butterfly. She turned it over and smiled at the date carved in the metal and lifted it for all to see.

"Thank you, men. I believe it's the loveliest gift I could ever receive. Look, Clive, they've put the date, so I'll always remember." Amos, standing behind her, took his handkerchief from his pocket and handed it to her, and she wiped her eyes. "Thank you, again. That was very kind, and I appreciate your gesture. Now, you best return to your duties, lest I be accused of fraternization with Marines young enough to be my sons."

Montrose would have laughed at the looks on

his men's faces, had not the situation been so somber. Instead, he took his sister's hand, lifted it to his lips and gave her a kiss, telling her, "To the most wonderful sister any man could ever have."

That brought a round of cheers from those around, providing both a good exit point for his men, as well as a distraction from his own moment in the limelight. It seemed a good way to begin the afternoon's activities, and he called to his sister and nephew, "Now, may we find a location to feed my hungry nephew?"

— 8 —

Lieutenant Clive Montrose, in full dress uniform, walked briskly down the boardwalk near the river, on his way to meet his nephew and his sister before they departed for Virginia. He could see the remnants of the visitors to the ceremony, the ladies dressed in their finest dresses, holding the arms of their men congregating near the storefronts. The men, military and civilian alike, turned to see him pass, whispering among themselves, but he ignored them in his haste. Suddenly, a man came up behind him, his breath coming in gasps.

"Sir! Lieutenant Montrose!" The man panted out his name above the sound of a wagon rolling by on the street. His felt hat was askew on his head, and his jacket had an ink stain on the front.

Montrose turned to see who would dare accost him on a public street. It was the reporter from the local newspaper, Abbott. With the shock of recognition, he remembered he had promised to give the man an interview for his paper.

"Damn." He blew out his cheeks and waited for the man to catch him. "I apologize for my haste. Did you still want the interview?"

The man grinned. "Oh, I took your advice. I had a most pleasant hour with Sergeant O'Malley. He was most helpful. My editor was pleased. I just wanted to congregate you on your award, sir. May I shake your hand?" He thrust out his fist, forgetful that he had a pencil in his fingers. They both laughed. Abbott withdrew his hand, put the pencil above his ear and shook hands with Montrose.

"Good-bye, sir. And, congratulations."

"Thank you, Abbott. You might want to do something about that stain on your jacket before it sets in permanently."

The reporter looked at his jacket, surprised, and turned, but Lieutenant Montrose was gone.

****

The train stood, waiting, its gray steam cloud rising in the still air

The day was quickly fading, with the sun just ducking behind the railway ticketing office in a blaze of orange and red sky. The evening shadows crept across the verdant grass covering the depot grounds, and the fading light obscured the railroad tracks leading out of town.

Now that the time had arrived, Montrose couldn't think of a word to say. It might be years before he chanced to see his sister and nephew again. She would return to Virginia, her husband and family; Amos would follow the Army wherever he was sent, for he had decided to make it his career.

As bits of polished brass on the massive engine caught the ruby sun, gleaming in the gathering gloom, the passengers began to embark, saying their last goodbyes to family and friends. The horn blew; the conductor yelled, "All aboard;" and Montrose took his sister in his arms.

"Take care and write to me. May God keep you safe," he whispered in her ear.

She stepped back, and Amos saluted and shook his hand. "It's been a good trip, Sir. I'll write when I can."

They walked to the train, and Amos helped his mother up the steps and followed her. They stood in the doorway one last time, waved, and disappeared from his sight. Several other passengers boarded the train, and he turned away. Trotter stood nearby with the buggy, holding the horse steady as the lonesome whistle blew, and the engine started forward. Montrose stood silently watching until the steel behemoth disappeared behind the buildings. With a heavy sigh, he stepped into the seat, his thoughts gloomy and deep. Trotter released the horse's reins from the post and paused a moment beside the wheel.

"Are you alright, Sir?"

Montrose looked at the younger man, his face

reddened from standing in the heat of the sun all day. His brown eyes looked concerned. He smiled. "Yes, Corporal Trotter, I'm alright."

He glanced down at the ribbon and medal on his uniform and started whistling an old Army tune as the buggy moved slowly out of town and toward the Marine station.

"Yes, Sir."

Montrose heard the corporal's soft reply, and in a moment Trotter joined him in his lively rendition of the song. His ordeal was over, and he was satisfied with the pleasant outcome of his sister's visit. He would return to his job as gun-division commander with a deeper commitment to the future. The sight of the tall masts of the sailing ships and the silhouettes of steam-driven gunboats in the harbor began to appear as they drew near the shore, and he stopped singing. A sense of pride and purpose filled his heart as his nostrils swelled with the scent of the sea breeze, the stench of dead fish and the odor of rotting vegetables. His two rooms in the officers' quarters were humble and bare, except for the essentials of life, but for now, they were home.

www.ingramcontent.com/pod-product-compliance
Lightning Source LLC
Chambersburg PA
CBHW071237260626
47159CB00005BA/1779